Cats, Cannolis and a Curious Kidnapping

An Anna Romano Mystery Series

Book One (2nd edition)

Cheryl Denise Bannerman

ISBN Print format: 978-1-7353352-2-3
ISBN Audio format: 9781662212895

Table of Contents

CHAPTER 1

Present Day

nna could not believe she had just stolen an ice cream cart from a little old man — *with a cane no less* — and was being chased by a deranged murderer. Just a few weeks ago, her life was PERFECTLY NORMAL.

She was definitely out of shape and now found herself wishing she had taken those spin classes her friend tried to sign her up for. All she could think about was stopping for a triple scoop, chocolate chip ice cream cone.

She was pedaling as fast as she could as she merged onto the local highway. Cars were honking their horns and kids were gawking and pointing at her through the windows. It was humiliating. For the first time in her life, she was hoping no one would recognize her.

Through the noise of the traffic she thought she heard laughter, and maybe even a catcall. She turned sharply, almost giving herself whiplash. She hadn't had a man 'call', let alone catcall, at her in quite some time. When she turned back around to focus on the road ahead, she saw in her peripheral view a man on a motorcycle. He was gesturing something to her, but she couldn't quite make out what he was saying. Then, out of nowhere, a gang of his motorcycle buddies pulled alongside him. They were all whistling, whooping, laughing, and ironically, yelling out ice cream orders.

Seconds later, they were moving closer to her lane, otherwise known as 'the shoulder', since there were *technically* no bike lanes on the highway. They then began gesturing for her to pull over!

Not looking where she was going, and becoming frantically nervous at the attention, Anna was caught off guard by a construction cone. She quickly swerved right to avoid it, but was too late.

Down the embankment she went, ice cream cart and all. Run off the road by a bunch of bikers who were craving Rocky Road. Damn.

She had to get to the police station, but had lost her main source of transportation. They were never going to believe this story.

Just 2 weeks ago...

Anna

Welcome to my life. My name is Anna Romano. I'm the lonely Italian lady from the shore. The Jersey Shore, that is. I now live in the suburbs of Central Jersey. The quaint, preppy town of Princeton to be exact. Thanks for reading about my exciting life of writing, cats, cooking, and kitty litter. I never thought I would turn into an old maid, unmarried, with seven cats at the age of 37, but here I am.

The most fulfilling part of my life is my work as an author. This is my fifteenth year in the world of fiction, specifically murder mysteries, and I love it. I get to work from home with my cats and don't have to deal with the politics of working in an office. I've always said that "death by cubicle" would be the worst death EVER. I could see myself stuck, almost frozen in time, listening to co-workers ramble on about their spouses, forging smiles through large arrays of kids' photos in various stages of life, and faking interest in slideshows of family vacations. Ugh!

In addition to writing novels, I also write from home part-time for the local newspaper's *Dear Jesse* relationship column. Honestly, this is the last topic I should be advising anyone on, but I manage to get by with my trademark sarcasm and sense of humor.

If I'm not on my laptop or cleaning litter boxes, I keep to myself watching the food and travel networks, trying my hand at new recipes, or watching scary movies.

It's not that I don't like people, I have just never been much of a social butterfly. I maintain a few close friends, *and even fewer family members*, in my circle. Most of them live out-of-state, visiting now and then. Our main way of staying touch is texting, which I don't mind, because if you get any of them on the phone it's hours before you can get them off. I also refuse to become a part of the social media culture, so my friends and family have made a habit of flooding my phone and inbox with photos of their happy families. I assume this is to prove to me that I am missing out on a large chunk of happiness in my life, and that I should hurry up and have a family before it's too late. God forbid!

I don't know why I haven't found the 'right one'. It could be (A) from a lack of trying, (B) my sarcasm and independence is a turnoff, or (C) I find most men annoying and harder to clean up after than my cats.

Maybe it is because I never saw any happy family scenarios growing up. Raised by a single parent, my mother was constantly bitching about life, work, and men; even though she was mildly successful and considered middle-class. She never married my dad and he wasn't around much anyway. Holidays and birthdays were his thing. He really showed out on those occasions with the gaudy presents and long hugs. I guess I should be grateful for that at least.

Mom was also a writer, but in the marketing industry, writing ads, commercials, and oftentimes jingles for the coolest kids' products on the market. It felt like Christmas when she was working on an ad campaign for a toy and had to bring it home for work. Mom was talented and creative, and I thank her for transferring that gift to me. Now living with her boyfriend of seven years, she resides in Texas and still works part-time for the same firm. I'm not sure how she ended up so far away, but it suits me fine. We talk weekly.

Dad passed away a few years back of a heart attack. It wasn't the wine or cigarettes that got him. It was, you guessed it, the women. Here's how it went…a prostitute, a drunk, and a pharmacist walk into a bar… Never mind, bad joke. Anyway, the blue pill was not recommended by his doctor and neither was the enthusiastic prostitute who wanted to 'try something different' that night. Dad's heart gave out during round two. He was a good man and did the best he could with what some refer to as 'the hand he was dealt'. Now that I think about it, I can see life being compared to a random game of cards, where 99.9% of the time, you lose. Hmph!

Regardless, let's get to the most important thing about my life that I know you are dying to hear about…my cats! There are seven in all: TatorTot, Tiny, Petra, Jasmine, Sonny, Liza, and Bette. I was on a Broadway kick when I picked the last few names. They keep me from thinking about my lack of a social life and their meowing helps to drown out the biological clock that, as everyone keeps telling me, is ticking *the older I get without a husband and family.*

TatorTot is my only Persian, mostly because of my allergies, and she is shy, gentle and quiet. Tiny, Sonny, and Petra are American Shorthair cats with unique stripes in various colors. Tiny is friendly and full of energy, while Sonny and Petra are the sneaky instigators who fight for my attention and can never seem to stay out of trouble. If they were kids, I can imagine one pointing to the other shouting, "He did it!" or "It wasn't me!" after getting caught in their latest conundrum.

Jasmine, the most entertaining of them all, is a black Siamese who loves to put on a show…especially when company comes over.

Then, there are Liza and Bette, my latest acquisitions. Two gorgeous ragamuffins who are literally inseparable. And no, despite their names, they are not the entertaining type like Jasmine. They love to eat, climb, jump, and type on my keyboard while I'm trying to work.

All of them have their own individual personalities, but they all seem to love eating and pooping based on the amount of litter I have to clean every day.

This just in! My publicist has texted me, "Don't be late tomorrow!"

One of the great things about my career is that I get to meet my fans at least three to five times a year at various events. My signing tomorrow is at the Rizzoli Bookstore in New York City for my latest book, *The Purrrfect Crime*. The premise: *A crime is committed by a veterinarian's assistant who catered to the animals of the rich and famous so she could get close to the families, kidnap their beloved pet, and demand a substantial ransom. After collecting millions, she was finally caught when the kidnapping of a prized Shih Tzu turned to murder. The maid's day off was changed at the last minute, and the owners caught the kidnapper off guard...*My animal lover fans ate it up and *The Purrrfect Crime* was on the bestseller list just two weeks after its release!

My publicist's name is Shirlene Booker, and yes, that is her actual last name. Her relatable passion for books has led to our now ten years of teamwork. The only thing she's more passionate about than books is public perceptions, which means bad punctuality is at the top of her list of pet peeves.

I texted her back: "Yes, SIR!"

There is a running joke between us that refers to her as having the bedside manner of a drill sergeant. Next, she will be asking what I am wearing. Oy vey!

I can't complain though. She's been by my side through thick and thin, and she always has my best interests at heart. Every time I push her too far and get on her last nerve about a venue or promotion, I just bake her a pan of my famous lasagna and all is well with 'The Booker' again.

Now to pick out the perfect spring outfit for my trip to the city tomorrow!

CHAPTER 3

Still 2 weeks ago...

Anna

The atmosphere is all abuzz as I step out of the town car that delivered me to my venue, twenty minutes early. Shirlene will be more than pleased at my punctuality.

There was already a crowd forming in the front of the store, which was a good sign. I made my way through the back entrance with my travel case on wheels in tow, and asked a clerk where my table was set up. He was happy to walk me to it, leading with a poised hand and an ear-to-ear grin — *as if he was a Price Is Right gal in a past life.*

I thanked him for his help, and was just unpacking my book copies, promo items, and pens when Shirlene popped up behind me, out of nowhere. "Well, look what the CAT dragged in! No pun intended!" she exclaimed jokingly.

I stood up to hug her and replied, "Hey, it's The Booker! You're looking well, as usual."

Shirlene replied, "Right back atcha, Superstar! I *love* that dress. I could never pull off flower prints, but you manage to do it with grace and beauty. You must share your fashion secrets with me, darrrrlinnnggg."

We were both having a good laugh when the manager interrupted to let us know they were going to begin letting folks in to start the signing in five minutes. Just enough time for me to tinkle and take my place.

Shirlene was already set to take her place at the front of the table. She was responsible for passing out promotional materials, gathering email addresses on the sign-in sheet for the marketing emails that went out bi-weekly, and handing out thousands of verbal 'thank you for comings'.

An hour into the event, I noticed a tall, wiry man with red hair in line to get his book signed. He seemed awfully nervous, biting his fingernails and furrowing his matching red eyebrows. When his turn came, he shuffled up to the table and said in a low voice, "I'd like you to dedicate this to my first wife, Cynthia. She was a big fan of yours…but she's dead now."

Now, I've met my share of weirdos, so at the time I just shrugged it off. But while signing, I did wonder why he would get an autograph for a dead woman. Creeeeepppppyyy.

I never mentioned the incident to Shirlene. And overall, the event was a success; we sold more books than expected, and got over 100 new names for our marketing list!

My feet were killing me, and I could not *wait* to get back into the town car and nap the whole ride home.

* * *

Waking up the day after a successful book signing had me in the mood to cook. I had been wanting to try a new recipe for chicken marsala and make some fresh cannoli. I could say I was making an extravagant meal expecting company, but honestly, that would be a lie. I just love to eat.

I headed out to the grocery store with my list of 70% cat food and cat supplies and 30% human food. It was a shopping ratio I was happy to accept. My babies love me unconditionally, *mostly because I feed them*. BUT they don't talk back or break my heart. In my opinion, it was the perfect relationship.

As I headed over to the deli counter, I saw a flash of red hair quickly pass by the aisle I was standing in. It reminded me of the tall, red-haired weirdo from the book signing. But that wouldn't make sense, unless the guy traveled all the way from Jersey to NYC for an autograph for his dead wife. Again, creeeeeppppppyyy.

I explained it away as bad vision from old age and kept shopping.

Checking out was a piece of cake today and I was in-and-out in no time. Although I preferred the older cashiers who were friendlier and more open to chitchat, I also enjoyed the younger generation who scanned as if they were in for the race of their life, with the bonus prize being a super long break where they could text, post, tweet, snap, and whatever else kids do nowadays. I must say though, it wouldn't kill them to pass along a simple hello or even a pleasant nod.

I was loading the trunk without noticing the carts going by in a whizz. Everyone rushing around in their busy lives with work, kids, and errands to fill up their day.

That's when I noticed a hand on my cart, which was soon firmly tightened around my wrist. I froze and looked up to see the red-haired man from the book signing. He looked me dead in the eyes and said, "Silence is golden, you know?" He then released my wrist and walked away. I was frozen in fear, unable to release any type of noise from my throat. Leaning back on my car for support, I looked around to see if anyone present had witnessed the *'interaction'*, for lack of a better word. It wasn't an assault, but he did grab my wrist for a few seconds. Should I report it? Since this was my second encounter with the man, I figured I should document something with the police in writing…just in case. I thought to tell Shirlene, but I didn't want to worry her for nothing.

I pulled up at the local police station and sat in the car for a minute to gather my nerve. I was sure this was more than a coincidence. Even if it wasn't, better safe than sorry.

I walked in and found the line for the check-in/info desk. The atmosphere made me feel as if I was signing up for government benefits or renewing my driver's license. I was third in line, and couldn't help thinking I should have unpacked the groceries first and then drove over. My dairy products may be melting while I stand here in line, and I can't imagine dinner being complete without the cannoli.

"Miss, may I help you?" a voice called out from a desk off to the side.

"Oh, yes. Sorry," I responded.

I told the officer I would like to file a report against someone I did not know in the least, for something that was not actually stalking or assault, and which could possibly be a coincidence or unrelated. I think he was as confused as I was.

He explained that the incident did not qualify as either stalking or assault, and basically told me to go home to my cats and take a valium. Apparently, he recognized me and knew of my neighborhood nickname, "The Author-Cat Lady", and wanted to get rid of me. Unfortunately, I was afraid that was exactly what the crazy red-haired man wanted to do as well.

But, if the police were blowing me off, what else could I do? Maybe I did need a valium.

1½ weeks ago...

Frederick Talon

The name's Frederic Talon. I never wanted any of this. If people would just learn to mind their own damn business. Everyone has secrets in their past…right?

I'm just your normal, mild-mannered, businessman trying to live the American dream. Wife, mortgage, two kids, and a dog. I maintained an okay job as a CPA. But somehow, it was never enough.

Growing up in a blue-collar household, both my parents worked their hands to the bone for the rich. My mother was a housekeeper, and my father a mechanic. They struggled to make ends meet in our small, two-bedroom apartment.

I was the puny kid with strange red hair that stood out in the poorer side of Bloomfield, New Jersey. Getting picked on for most of my life, as a teen I couldn't wait to get a job in Montclair, the next town over. I was able to buy nicer clothes and even started dating, albeit a bit awkwardly. With my confidence multiplied by ten, I came out of my shyness and was much more confident in all areas of my life…except when it came to girls.

My parents managed to save up enough for me to attend the local college and I got my degree in accounting. Numbers were my thing and I was pleased with my decision to become an accountant. I had always dreamed of having my own company and working for myself.

My dreams fell to the wayside when I met my first wife during a business trip to Connecticut. She was dominant, vocal, and not one for compromise. I found it exciting *at first*, especially in the bedroom, but then I realized if I heard her say, "Freddy baby, now you know that's not what we agreed on", one more time I would lose it. We never *agreed* to anything. It was HER way or NO way. No in-between.

She thought it was too risky to start my own business, and just wanted me to take a secure corporate job with a stable salary. My dreams were crushed.

Just when I thought her complaining would be the death of me, she succumbed to a tragic end. It happened at a time when we were trying to conceive. The doctors suspected she had a severe reaction to the fertility treatments and the sickness just took over. By the time she got to the hospital, it was too late. I was burying her a week later. I was devastated that we would never have a chance to bring a life into this world. I truly loved her, but I have to admit, the silence was golden.

Now here I am with wife number two and, once again, the nagging never stops, wanting me to do more, have more, give more time…Ugh! How much can one man take?

It's bad enough my wife's 'daddy' runs the chain of accounting firms that I work for and is filthy rich. He also happens to be a self-righteous, entitled prick who was born with a silver spoon in his mouth; which makes for the worst type of boss – and father-in-law.

If it wasn't for the twins and the pre-nup my wife made me sign, I would have tried to get out long ago. My boys, however, are the joy of my life, with bright fiery red hair, just like their daddy. Coming out of my first marriage without children was a disappointment, so I was cherishing any time with my boys. It was exciting watching them reach the various milestones: crawling, walking, and eventually running. They're now getting ready to enter the fourth grade.

Driving from the shore back to the suburbs of North Jersey gave me the time I needed to finalize my plan. Hopefully my message was received loud and clear. I don't believe in coincidences, and there is no way this woman could know this much about my past.

I now have the solution to having it all. My wife will die tragically in a boating accident, which I have planned for the upcoming summer break with the family. I stand to inherit millions based on the insurance policy payout on accidental deaths. But right now, I just couldn't help but worry.

Everything was going as planned…until that stupid book lady. She could ruin everything! Damn her!

Anyway, for now, I have to get inside to work. I'm already late and the boss…*Knock, knock, knock!*

A persistent pair of knuckles rapped on my car window. Knuckles that happened to be connected to the arm of the self-righteous, entitled prick, otherwise known as my father-in-law.

"Frederick! What the hell? I've been looking for you all morning!" he barked.

"Sorry, sir. I had some medical stuff to take care of. I thought I sent you an email yesterday, sir." I responded like a nervous teenage boy going through puberty. The old man always seemed to have that effect on me.

"Well, get in there and get to work! You sure can't accomplish anything from the damn parking lot, now can ya?" he barked yet again.

As we rode the elevator together in silence, I thought about the night before and the exhilaration I felt right before I said those two magic words that drained me of my last grand… *"Hit Me."*

The dealer had a slight smirk on his face as he said, "Busted, house wins", in what seemed to be slow motion.

Driving down to the shore to check out that book lady had exposed me to the best of Atlantic City's sites, which included all of the casinos along the shore. I must have hit five or six before I tapped out. After losing a bet on the Giants game last

Sunday, I was beginning to sweat a little more than usual. The ding of the elevator snapped me out of my daydream, and I headed to my desk.

Time to make the donuts.

CHAPTER 5

1 week ago...

Anna

"Hello...helloooooo!" No answer again from the other end of the line. These crank calls are really getting on my nerves. I wish they'd at least breathe heavily and say something inappropriate to get me started! Leaving me hanging is just cruel, and probably the closest thing I'll get to a date for a while.

In all seriousness, this week has been hell. Besides the crank calls, I've been hearing noises at night, getting strange anonymous emails, and I swear I'm being followed every time I go out.

Speaking of going out, I should actually be on my way out right now. I had better grab the gift and the pan of cannoli I baked last night and head over to my friend Bonnie's house, who lives in the next town over.

Bonnie and I met at the newspaper I work for part-time. She's having a baby shower for her third kid. Frankly, I think that voluntarily putting yourself through childbirth after the first time shouldn't warrant a party. I mean, really, I've seen the childbirth videos. Who chooses to do that? Insane!

Driving through the suburban neighborhoods with their perfectly landscaped lawns and expensive cars in the driveways makes me cringe. I can only imagine the mortgage and utility bills, all for a big home to parade around to friends. Although, my babies would surely have a field day with over 2,000 square feet of home to run around in.

I pulled into the driveway of Bonnie's home, and was greeted by her husband Dave and their two kids. They hugged me, grabbed the gift and tray of cannoli, and ran ahead of me to announce my arrival. I was officially marked present. Now I would spend the next few hours answering questions about my next book, why I am not dating, and why I don't want children. An Italian woman who could cook and had no man or children was an oxymoron to them. However, I couldn't hear any of it because of that damn biological clock. Shut up already, will ya?!

Three hours later, I loaded myself into the car with just my pocketbook, feeling a bit shortchanged, when I got a text message from a strange number. It simply said, "Drive safe". I texted back, "Who is this?" but there was no response.

I don't mind a little mystery in my life, but this was getting ridiculous.

I decided to call Shirlene and get some insight.

She answered on the first ring. Since I had her on hands-free, her greeting echoed through the car and startled me more than usual.

"Hey Superstar! What's shakin'?" she rang in.

"Oh, just coming from a friend's baby shower where I was grilled for hours about not having a family, and kindly informed about how my time was almost up to do so. You would think I was dying or something. Maybe I'll want kids when I'm older. I've seen women on the news having miracle babies in their mid-forties!"

Shirlene roared with laughter and said, "Yeah sure, except it's called artificial insemination…without a man!"

"Haha, very funny. I could easily get a man and go on a date if I so chose, thank you very much!" I responded.

"Of course you could, you're a gorgeous Italian who can cook her 'cannoli' off! Any man's dream!" she said.

"Yeah, yeah, anyway, I'm calling to see if you remember the weird red-haired guy from the book signing in New York?" I asked, changing the subject away from my uterus.

Shirlene didn't seem to know who I was referring to.

I went on with my story explaining the weird type of altercation in the grocery store, the crank calls, and strange text messages and emails.

"What the hell does 'silence is golden' mean? What a freak! Did you tell the cops?" Shirlene asked, apparently growing agitated and concerned.

I explained the laughter at the police station when I tried, which seemed to upset her even more.

"Nobody messes with my Superstar! I'm headed to your house this evening and we can work out a plan, okay?" she dictated.

"No Shirlene, you don't have to do that. I just wanted to tell you what was going on. Just in case, you know? And, now that I am saying it aloud, the whole scenario sounds utterly ridiculous. I'm sure I am just being overly paranoid as usual. I'll keep you informed if anything else happens, I promise," I pleaded.

A calmer Shirlene responded, "Okay, luv. But you promise to call me, and the cops, if this freak tries to take 'crazy' to the next level?"

"Absolutely! I'll call you a bit later. Thanks, Shirlene!" Hitting the disconnect button, I wondered what the next level would be.

* * *

As I pulled into the driveway and opened the garage door, I anticipated seeing Petra or Tiny running to the window. But nothing.

I closed the garage and walked through the door that led to the kitchen and still, nothing. No one was running to greet me or brushing up and down my legs. Where was everyone?

That's when I saw it, turning the corner into the living room. The entire wall was desecrated. Smeared with photographs of me at the grocery store, outside the house gardening, driving…it was so eerie I got a cold chill up my spine and the little hairs on the back of my neck stood upright to attention. Right above the photos, in red paint, were the words "SILENCE IS GOLDEN." His message was clear. The tall, wiry man with the red hair wanted me to remain silent about something…but what?

This was definitely *'the next level'*. Shirlene was right, as usual.

Remembering why I was headed to the living room in the first place, I looked down in search of my babies. There was a sinking feeling in the pit of stomach when I saw the first drop of red on the carpet. I was convincing myself it was just a drop of paint, when I saw the second drop…

I covered my mouth with my hand and held my breath. There is no way anyone could be that cruel. I followed the drops down the hallway until the trail stopped in front of the linen closet. I could feel my hands trembling as I reached for the knob and turned it slowly clockwise. The closet door was only open a crack when the seven of them ran out in a panic. Oh, thank God! Distressed meows and loud purring ensued as I bent down to hug them all. My life was nothing without these guys. They were my family and I loved them. In that moment I was beyond thankful the stalker had a conscience, or heart, or whatever made sickos like this tick. In the end, he decided to spare my babies.

I knew this was the last straw. I could not dismiss this incident. Unlike a crank call, this type of invasion into my life threatened my safety and the safety of my babies. This could not be taken lightly.

I dialed 911 and waited.

30 minutes later, my doorbell rang. Tiny was the only one who ran for the door. I scooped him up so he wouldn't make a run for it, and welcomed the officers inside.

"Ma'am. You called about a break-in?" said the younger officer with the five o'clock shadow. Either he had just pulled a double or he thought that look was sexy on him. It wasn't.

"Come in please. Yes, I called," I responded politely, *hoping he could not read my thoughts about his scruffy face.*

"My name is Detective Jim Billings, and this is Detective John Solace. Let's start from the beginning. When did you notice the break-in? Was anything taken?"

I recounted my story of returning home less than an hour ago from a friend's house and guided them into the living room to view the wall. I then told them about the crank calls, strange noises, concerning anonymous emails and text messages, and the feeling that I was being followed every time I go out. When they asked if there was anyone I suspected, I told them the story of the tall, wiry man with the red hair, the encounter in the grocery store parking lot, and how the local police would not take my initial report. I left out the part of the story that included sarcasm and laughter on the part of several officers, as I had no desire of getting anyone in trouble.

I also told the officers I had no idea who the man was and what he wanted me to stay silent about. It appeared to be just as baffling to them as it was to me. The older detective gave me his card and recommended I invest in a security system. I had never given a security system a second thought after all these years in this quiet neighborhood, but apparently *times were a-changin'.*

I locked up tight after they left and made the call to the security company I just recently saw a commercial for. Their jingle was stuck in my head and I definitely needed to get the ball rolling on this. The safety of my family is a top priority and if I can't feel safe in my own home, where could I feel safe?

After I confirmed the appointment for the next morning and got everyone fed, I pulled out my laptop and set up a new document for a brainstorming session. I had to figure out why I was being targeted by this man.

Description of man: 6'2", red hair, Caucasian, thin, slightly balding, pale complexion, wireframe glasses

Location: Met in NYC at booksigning, but could possibly live in NJ

Status: Widowed, Wife's name = Cynthia, was a fan of my books

Suspects:

- Anyone with a grudge.

- A rival author angry about one of my books.

- Someone I gave advice to in my *Dear Jesse* column that is upset with me. Maybe I told a wife to leave her husband or boyfriend, and he was seeking revenge.

NOTE: Low probability for #3: I am anonymous in my column and no one knows my real name.

As I scanned my brainstorming notes, I noticed the same word pop up several times...*book*. What could he think I knew, that he needed me to, in his words, *stay silent* about? Something about this man reminded me of a character from one of my past books, *The Silent Kill*. It was the story of a jewel thief who killed his mistress to keep her quiet, after she stumbled upon his criminal late-night activities. But how could this man and a fictional character in a story be related?

I knew what I was looking for was bigger than Google, so I headed to the only place I knew for **real** answers...the library.

Before I headed out, I texted Shirlene: *"You were right. He leveled up. Call you later."*

* * *

Upon entering the library, I headed straight for the Reference section. The library closes in two hours, so I would have to work fast.

The first step would be to gather the date, location and any other pertinent information from the killer in my book, along with what I knew about my red-haired stalker, so I can narrow the search. I came up with the following: *2011, Connecticut, Cynthia, mistress, murder, poison.*

The killer in my book used a poison that mimicked a heart attack and the coroner never suspected a thing. I did a lot of medical research on this poison and thought it was the perfect escape plan for a criminal. I pulled up my notes from my laptop to refresh my memory:

"Digitoxin is a cardiac glycoside. It has similar structure and effects to digoxin (though the effects are longer-lasting). Unlike digoxin (which is eliminated from the body via the kidneys), it is eliminated via the liver, so could be used in

patients with poor or erratic kidney function. However, it is now rarely used in current Western medical practice. While several controlled trials have shown digoxin to be effective in a proportion of patients treated for heart failure, the evidence base for digitoxin is not as strong, although it is presumed to be similarly effective. Digitoxin exhibits similar toxic effects to the more commonly used digoxin, namely: anorexia, nausea, vomiting, diarrhea, confusion, visual disturbances, and cardiac arrhythmias. Antidigoxin antibody fragments, the specific treatment for digoxin poisoning, are also effective in serious digitoxin toxicity."

Source: http://www.3dchem.com/Digitoxin.asp

I was beginning to feel like one of the detectives on *Law and Order* and had the theme song playing in my head as I walked in slow motion to the microfiche machine… until I was rudely interrupted.

"Miss, excuse me, miss?" a small elderly woman with a crackly voice spoke as she reached out for my hand. "You have to sign up for the machines up front and the time allotted is one hour per session, unless no one is waiting. Also, we are closing very soon."

I nodded my head and smiled, as I internally rolled my eyes and headed for the Information Desk at the front of the library.

After signing up and being explained the rules very slowly by yet another elderly library worker, I headed back to my 'case' at hand. The theme song was playing again in my head as I walked.

Typing in my key words, I was sure the results would punish me with a dozen or more rolls of film to sift through, but the number was only three. I quickly wound the film and began scrolling. After an hour, I was beginning to see double when I came across an article that made me take notice…

A man who bore a striking resemblance to my stalker was suspected of having something to do with his wife's death in 2011 in Connecticut. Her death was eventually ruled accidental. Could this be my stalker? The resemblance was uncanny, so I referred back to my notes.

> Description of man: 6'2", red hair, Caucasian, thin, slightly balding, pale complexion, wireframe glasses

Pieces of the puzzle were coming together in my head. Based on the article:

The man's name was Frederick Talon. He lived in Connecticut with his wife and had no kids. Following the wife's death, the coroner announced no evidence of foul play or toxins in her system. It was therefore not ruled a homicide, but it was noted that the local authorities had a hunch Frederick somehow got away with murder.

Maybe it was just one of those hunches cops sometimes had — like sexy TV detective, Elliot Stabler. However, most of the hunches he had got him into hot water with the captain.

There were some very distinguishable differences between this man and my fictional book character though. This Frederick Talon guy didn't kill his mistress, there was no mistress, and he certainly didn't appear to be a sophisticated jewel thief. He looked more like a malnourished book nerd with no fashion sense.

Yet, he must think I know something about him that could hurt him in some way. He wants me to stay silent for a reason, right? I have to find this man and notify the police of the name

I found in the article. Or maybe I should go to the police *first*, since this guy is obviously *off his rocker*.

I rushed out of the library with a new sense of purpose and pulled out of the parking lot headed for the police station.

While driving, I couldn't help but wonder if that handsome older officer who gave me his card, would be working on my break-in case. I think his name was Solace…John Solace. What a great name. Similar to Bond…James Bond. While imagining him saying his name in slow motion and slowly removing the handcuffs from his belt…

Beeeeeeeeeeeeeeeeeeeepppppppp!!!! "Watch it, lady!" a road-raged man screamed at me for drifting into his lane.

I waved apologetically and ditched my fantasy for another day. I had a stalker, possible murderer, to catch!

* * *

Traffic was a nightmare late in the evening. Everyone rushing home to either the loneliness of an empty apartment or a spouse and kids that made them crazy and miserable. To avoid the chaos, I decided to take the back roads to the police station.

I was singing along to my favorite Elton John song when I realized I was approaching a four-way stop intersection and prepared to brake. But the brakes were not working for some reason. I instantly began panicking because cars were crossing the intersection at a steady pace. I was left with only one option to avoid a catastrophe…*stop the car myself*.

I studied the wooded area to my right, ensured my seat belt was secure, pulled as hard as I could on the emergency brake for good luck, and yanked the wheel sharply to the right before I got to the intersection. Thank God I was only going about 30 mph. After several dips and swipes across many branches and shrubs, the car came to a stop. I said a gazillion *Hail Marys* and slowly undid my seat belt.

I don't understand how this happened. The car was *just* serviced last week, so did someone tamper with my brakes? Or am I becoming paranoid? More paranoid than usual that is.

Oh crap! I just remembered what I forgot to do last month from my *rarely reviewed* to-do list. I forgot to renew my annual membership for roadside assistance. Well, when one door closes, another one opens! Time to call Detective Solace for help. I peeked in the mirror to check my hair, clothes, and makeup before pulling his card out of my wallet.

After giving myself a quick wink and smile, I closed the mirror and dialed the detective who had invaded my earlier handcuff fantasy.

"Hello, may I speak to Detective James, I mean John…Solace please," I inquired of the deep and authoritative voice on the phone.

"Yeah, just a sec," he barked.

After a series of clicks and beeps, I was transferred to Detective Solace's voicemail. "This is Detective Solace. Sorry I cannot take your call. Leave a detailed message after the beep."

Crap! Voicemail. I'm terrible at leaving messages and I was super nervous, so I went in quick and fast with my re-introduction, car troubles, and recent research, but was stopped short by a good Samaritan.

It went something like this:

"I don't know if you remember me, my name is Anna Romano and you came to my house about the break-in. There was vandalism, and my cats were traumatized, and the red paint turned out not to be blood, thank God, and you gave me your card. Anyway, I think someone tampered with my brakes and I've crashed on the side of the road on the way from the library to your office. However, I have some very important information about the man with the red hair, it's related to…one sec a good Samaritan has finally stopped to help me. Thank goodness!"

He was wearing a hat pulled down low on his face with an oversized Giants jersey and faded blue jeans, so she couldn't see his face, but he looked just like…

"Oh goodness, this can't be happening. Please, don't hurt me…my cats!"

The line went dead.

Still a week ago...

Detective Solace

I stepped away for ten minutes and already have a voicemail. Geez. I dialed the code to access my message as I adjusted the name plaque on my desk: Det. J. Solace. When I was younger, I was told my last name stood for peace and comfort, but once I graduated high school, my life was anything but peaceful, or comforting for that matter. I bounced from job to job, my mom got sick, my brother was in and out of jail, and I had no idea which direction my life was going. I finally found my direction when I decided to enter the academy at 27. But being a cop on the beat in Newark proved more than I could handle, so I put in for a transfer further south, in the university town of Princeton.

However, there seems to never be a dull moment around here either. I thought a small town would be quiet and uneventful; a nice place to start over and put the past behind me. But that wasn't the case at all.

I played back voicemail message number one and my jaw dropped.

What the…?! Looks like the cat lady's stalker has just added kidnapping to his list of skills. She's in big trouble!

I know exactly where that intersection is located.

"Billings, you're with me!" I yelled across the squad room anxiously.

"Yes sir!" Billings replied. Billings is a rookie and a bit rough around the edges, but he's an okay guy.

After looking up the make and model of Ms. Romano's car, I instructed Billings to grab the keys and get CSU to meet us at the Four Points intersection just a couple of miles up the road. Maybe we would get lucky and find a fingerprint on the car.

While Billings was driving, I was on the phone trying to get the number to the local library.

"Sir, I can see the car in that ditch off to the right." Billings pointed with one hand steadying the wheel.

"Perfect, let's see what we got!" I replied, as Billings pulled over and came to a stop.

I could not believe the luck this poor woman was having. She seemed nice enough and was supposedly a well-known author. So, why was this guy hassling her? I remember the heavenly aroma coming from her house, like she had just finished baking something and I thought…

"Sir, you okay?" Billings was asking me something.

"Yes, I'm fine," I responded, pulling myself back to the present.

"Sir, I was asking if you could smell that. It's coming from the driver's side seat." Billings frustratingly asked for the second time.

I immediately recognized the smell. The perp must have used chloroform to subdue her and transferred some of it to the leather seat.

"Wait for CSU and have them test the seat for trace chemicals and fingerprints on the windows and doors. Inside and out. You got it?" I barked and saw Billings roll his eyes as he walked away.

This case was getting to me. Even though I wasn't the one to blow her off the first time she tried to ask for help, I felt guilty, and would feel even guiltier if something happened to her. This was now officially a kidnapping case.

The library was not picking up their phone. Ugh! Screw calling on the phone, I had to get to the library and figure out what she discovered. I yelled out to Billings that I was taking the car and to wait here for CSU.

The sight of the library brought up one of my best college memories. It was a library just like this where I met my wife. I was a football jock and she was a beautiful genius. An awkward match made in heaven, but just perfect to me.

Martha was one-of-a-kind. Studying to be a molecular biologist, she was ambitious, smart, articulate and absolutely breathtaking. The most beautiful thing about her was that she was completely oblivious to her beauty, wondering often why men made such a fuss over her and wondering what they saw in a homely nerd like her. You don't find humility like that in women today. To be honest, I don't see many traits at all that appeal to me in today's female gene pool.

I looked at my watch and realized they may be closed as I approached the glass doors. As if on cue, a woman with her hands full of bags and books came through the doors with a large keyring. Damn!

I flashed my badge and my best smile and told her what I needed, with my fingers crossed behind my back. She then went into a long story about how Ms. Romano tried to use the machine without signing in and then rolled her eyes at her when she told her they were closing soon.

I reiterated that time was of the essence, as this is now a missing person's case and that I would greatly appreciate a few extra minutes of her time this evening.

After a lot of sighs and recounts of the many errands on her list to be completed before getting home to her family, she re-opened the door, entered the code to silence the alarm she had *just* set, and rebooted the main computer.

After accessing the history from the computer Ms. Romano used earlier, it seems she researched the following terms: *2011, Connecticut, Cynthia, mistress, murder, and poison.* She was scrolling through 2011 news feeds when she pressed PRINT on a news article about a man who was suspected of killing his wife in 2011 in Connecticut. The librarian headed to the back to locate the film and returned with a printed copy of the same article.

I thanked her profusely and scurried out the door with my cell in hand. "Billings, how's it going?" I rattled off into the phone.

"Going great! CSU is here and they were able to confirm the chemical on the seat was chloroform, and lifted two partial prints from the door handle and window," he responded proudly. "How's it going on your end, sir?"

"I was able to get the information on her research from the library, but it makes no sense. I have a hunch about something, so I'm going to need the car a bit longer than expected. Are you okay getting a lift back to the station?" I asked.

"No problem, sir. Let me know if you need anything else," Billings responded kindly.

Now, to find evidence supporting my hunch. I couldn't just go harass a complete stranger just because someone printed an article with them in it.

I hoped Ms. Romano hadn't installed that alarm system we recommended yet, or I'd have to answer to the Sarge for breaking and entering. And what about all those cats? Do cats attack intruders? I don't have much experience with cats.

I pulled up just as the porch light was coming on. It must have been on a sensor or timer. It was getting dark and I was starting to really worry about the safety of the victim. Every hour she was missing proved more and more dangerous for her.

I was checking the doors and windows in the front of house, smiling and waving nicely at the cats giving me the stink eye in the front window, when a voice startled me from behind.

"Is Anna okay? I saw your police car outside from my front window," an elderly man asked from his motor scooter on the sidewalk below.

Flashing my badge to make the man feel more comfortable, I responded, "No sir, Ms. Romano is missing, and we need to get into her home to gather clues to help find her."

"Oh, that's just awful. Don't cops usually use that heavy door blaster thingy to knock doors down?" he asked.

"You mean a battering ram? No sir. Only SWAT uses those for raids. We wouldn't want to damage a victim's property," I answered.

"Well, in that case, you may want to just use the key." The man pointed to a flowerpot to the right of the porch, in front of the rose bushes.

I couldn't believe it was that simple, or that people still put spare keys under items on their front lawn in plain view. Incredible! I thanked the man and he rolled away, mumbling something or other.

As I entered the home, I didn't hear any beeping, so I assumed the alarm company hadn't been out yet. I turned my attention to the ongoing rubbing on my legs going on down below. Apparently, they don't attack, they just rub. While trying to concentrate, the cats purring was getting incessantly louder, so I decided to check their food and water.

I wasn't expecting to end up feeding and scooping the poop of Ms. Romano's cats, but it was the least I could do. We, the department, had failed her and I have to make it right. Luckily, while I was in the kitchen, I just happened to find the source of the sweet aroma from the other day, and helped myself to a couple of cannoli. Yummmm!

I was ready to get down to business and headed for the bookcase. First, I located her laptop, but was unable to log in without her password. Next, I located all of her novels and brought them with me to the recliner in the living room. As I began skimming through each one trying to find the connection between this kidnapping and a man who murdered his wife in 2011 in Connecticut, cannoli-itis rudely set in and I dozed off to sleep to the soft caress of fur and a gentle purring in my ear.

CHAPTER 7

6 days ago...

Anna

Ugh, my head. Where the heck was I? The cement below me was cold and damp. It smelled of stale sweat and urine, and there were old swatches of colorful materials and broken-down sewing machines scattered about. An old sweatshop or factory maybe?

The ropes that bound my hands and feet were tied and knotted very well. What was this guy, a boy scout in his youth? They were chafing the heck out of my wrists and ankles and I could see purple marks beginning to appear.

A noise came from the other room and I saw him through the glass panes used to create some form of privacy for what seemed to be an office. Red Head (his new nickname) was finishing up an argument on the phone with someone about a missing cadaver, and was now opening the door and heading my way.

"What do you want from me?" I tried to scream, although it was useless through the gag in my mouth. Once Red Head appeared in full view, I quickly noted the shiny silver item in his right hand and quieted. He was now holding the gun to my head. *What had I gotten myself into?*

"You think you are so clever, don't you? With your 'fictional' mystery books that appear to be so innocent!" Red Head yelled.

I tried to respond but to no avail. That was when he reached for the gag, put the gun closer to my head, and offered to remove the gag *if* I didn't scream.

I nodded profusely in agreement.

As soon the gag was removed, I entered my plea. "Listen, the stories in my books are just mere figments of my imagination. I don't know anything about you or your life. You have to believe me!"

"No, I don't," he responded slowly and smiled slyly. "It just so happens your meddling is going to fit into my plan perfectly."

"Did you know that you just happen to be the *perfect* victim? No spouse, no social life, just cats. Only your cats will miss you. And your book fans, of course," he spat and chuckled simultaneously. "Just think, your books will be even more valuable when you're dead. You'll be a legend!" he laughed aloud.

I could not believe what I was hearing. I never thought my life would end over the thing that I loved most…writing. One of my very own books had set the wheels in motion towards my demise. I had to find a way to get out of this. Where was Detective Solace? Was he even looking for me? And what will happen to my babies? They must be hungry and scared, me being gone for so long?

I had almost forgotten the one person who brought me into this world… miserable as it may be. My mother. She did her best to give me a good life, although she was not around much. I have the most painful memories of birthdays. From eight until sixteen years of age, sitting in my favorite Italian restaurant having my favorite meal, with a beautiful pink cake lit up with pink candles. As I stared off into space, the staff sang happy birthday and clapped. My mother would set the whole thing up, but was never present. I was surrounded by strangers who I knew little about.

I would open my presents from her and then anxiously wait by the front window for her to pick me up. On my sixteenth birthday she decided I was old enough to catch a taxi home. After that birthday, I was determined to have friends and make a life for myself, so that I would never have to be alone again. Hence, the seven cats…but I digress.

Just then, as if sensing the sad story in my head was over, Red Head glanced at me over his right shoulder with a softer look on his face. His back was to me, the gun still in his right hand as he said, "I'm sorry, Cat Lady. I really am. But this is the only solution I have to save my wife and children."

Still 6 days ago...

Detective Solace

I awoke, startled, in a coughing fit. I think I have a hairball in my throat. [more hacking] What time is it? 5:19 am? Oh crap! I gotta wrap up this research and check in with Billings. I dialed his cell and waited for him to pick up.

Last night, I deduced the novel, *The Silent Kill*, was the closest match to the article Ms. Romano had stumbled upon. The guy's name was Frederick Talon, but he didn't kill his mistress or his wife. Actually, his first wife died of natural causes. It was determined no foul play was even involved.

Billings answered on the fifth ring, mid-yawn, and I asked him to run the name Frederick Talon through CODIS and see if we can get a match to any of the partial prints we found on or inside Ms. Romano's vehicle.

After feeding the little ones and emptying their litter boxes again, I raced home to shower and change. As I was applying my daily moisturizing products, *aftershave and a dollop of hair mousse*, my cell phone chirped. A message from Billings. Finally!

I snatched up the phone and read the message:

Fingerprints match Frederick Talon. Ran credit card - charges at local h/w store for duct tape, rope, tarp. Search warrant appvd. Meet us at 721 Ravenhurst Lane.

I grabbed my belt, holster and badge and flew out the door. Plugging the address into my GPS, I thought about Ms. Romano. Such a nice lady. I had to find her. I needed to find her…alive.

* * *

"What do we have Billings?" I asked as I vested up outside the home.

"SWAT has two in the back, two on the side of the house, and two waiting for you to go in the front, sir," he responded.

"Let's move in!" I shouted, managing a countdown on three fingers, right hand in the air.

The front door was rammed off the hinges and we all moved in, both front and back reinforcements.

From all around the house you heard, "Clear…clear," until the final unit checked in. "All clear!"

I'm confused. If this is the family home, where was the family? There were no cars in the garage, no toys laying around, no dishes in the sink. Did this guy harm his family in some way? We couldn't find any clues whatsoever in this five-bedroom, three-bath home. Time to canvas the neighborhood.

Billings and I were only on our third house, when a neighbor, apparently an avid member of the Neighborhood Watch, provided us with the answers we needed. Apparently, they went away for the kid's summer break two days ago with approximately five suitcases, and wouldn't be back until the end of August. He also proceeded to tell us about the noticeable curves in Mrs. Talon's body and how she watered the rose bushes every Tuesday, Thursday, and Saturday right out front, in the most scandalous of outfits. Better add this guy to my radar. He was a bit *too* perceptive.

Anyway, back to business…how in the world did Anna fit into a family trip? It's not like he could bring her along and pretend she was just a friend from work or something. And if he didn't bring her along, where was he hiding her?

This case was making less and less sense the more we investigated. A wealthy family, a random cat lady/author, a sudden penchant for violence from a boring accountant and family man.

"Sir, we have a list of those properties you asked for," Billings addressed me as he leaned in to show me a printout.

"Looks like he purchased an old warehouse sometime last year. Maybe he was thinking of opening an office downtown? Maybe break away from Daddy Dearest with his own accounting firm?"

"Let's check it out," I said to Billings with a nod as I tossed him the car keys.

5 days ago...

Frederick Talon

I never thought this day would come. I have to get Cat Lady to the lake house and get everything else set up on the boat. I've been running through the checklist over and over in my mind:

Drug Cat Lady…check!

Move body to lake house…check!

Plant cadavers on the boat…check!

Disappear…check!

The family was already at the lake house and the new identities and accounts were all set up. Thank goodness the smaller cadavers from the university were delivered yesterday and already at the house.

I just have to give her lunch and then get her into the trunk. It should only take a few drops of morphine in her soup and sandwich meal from the corner deli. She hasn't eaten for a whole day, so she's probably starving by now. Meaning, she will be out quick, making my job even easier. I need her as quiet as possible until I arrive at the lake house to be with my family one last time. Thank goodness she's a petite lady, making her easy to lift and carry.

Thirty minutes later, I was pulling onto the highway when my cell phone rang. I pressed 'Answer' on the GPS screen and a deep voice filled the car. "Runnin' ain't gonna save you or your family, Freddy boy. This is your last warning. You know what you need to do." The call ended.

I sure did. The time had finally come to act. My whole life people walked all over me, telling me what to do, what to wear, what to eat. Even with my first wife, I NEVER had a voice. NO MORE! ALL OF THAT WILL END VERY SOON! I'LL BE THE NEW MAN ON TOP!

* * *

Scraps of duct tape, a length of rope, an empty syringe, and an empty bag from Ryan's Deli down the street was all that remained in the warehouse when the police arrived.

The trail in the hunt for Ms. Romano had just gone cold...again. She had definitely been held here, but the kidnapper had decided to move her again. Where was he headed? And, where was his damn family?! How many bodies would the police find before this case was all over?

Still 5 days ago...

Frederick Talon

Something didn't feel right. I thought the plan was running smoothly until I was headed home to shower and change and saw the officer outside the house. Why would there be an officer on my street?

I didn't want to take a chance, so I just kept going. It was a long drive to the lake house. Switching cars with one of my co-workers was a brilliant idea, if I do say so myself. The perfect ruse.

I was almost home free. Just stay calm (I told myself). Don't start getting paranoid now.

Thank goodness that pain-in-the-ass author is still knocked out in the trunk from the morphine, I thought, as I began to bear right at the exit ramp towards the popular boating community.

Yep, almost home free.

That's when I saw them. The red and blue lights in my rear-view mirror.

"Shit!" I said aloud as a loud, echoing, electronic voice urged me to pull over immediately.

I was sweating profusely when the officer approached my window and tapped lightly for me to lower it.

"You know why I stopped you, right?"

I played dumb and shrugged my shoulders in confusion.

"You have a broken taillight and you were fiddling with your cell phone when you passed me. That's a new violation in this state. License and registration please," the officer demanded.

Almost stuttering, I responded, "Ye-, ye-, yes sir, right here sir," as I handed him my ID and insurance card. How could I have missed that taillight when I borrowed her car?! So stupid!

I was drenched in sweat as the officer examined my credentials and my face in detail. I may have to change my shirt *and pants* when all this was said and done. I was just waiting for him to notice the name on the insurance card, my co-worker's husband's name did not match mine.

Finally, the officer headed back to his patrol car, but stopped abruptly at the trunk of the car. His head was cocked slightly to the side.

"Sir, I'm going to need you to step out of the vehicle and hand over the keys, so I can examine the trunk. NOW!" the officer shouted.

I did as I was told, handing the keys over to him slowly. He then forced me against the side of the car and handcuffed my hands behind my back. I had no idea what I was going to do if he found the author lady.

I was almost home free. Now it was all coming to an end.

The officer pressed the trunk release button and it lifted only slightly. Cautiously, he walks over to open it with his gun drawn.

Just then, his radio squawks a 187 at a bank robbery in progress down the street. "OFFICER DOWN! ALL UNITS RESPOND!"

I was back in the game! YES!

The officer quickly put away his gun, uncuffed me, handed me my keys, looked me dead in the eyes, and issued a stern warning to stay off the phone and get the taillight fixed as soon as possible.

As I watched him speed off, sirens blaring, I stood on the side of the road in shock. Snapping out of my trance only seconds later, I shut the trunk and took off for the house once again.

Yes, the plan was back in motion.

CHAPTER 11

Still 5 days ago...

Detective Solace

I held my cell phone close to his face and asked, "Have you seen this man, sir?"

"Oh yeahhhh, I seent dat guy! Came in now and nen for the *soup and sandwich* combo," he responded.

Judging by the accent, this guy was a New York native laying down his family roots in Jersey.

"When was the last time you saw him?" I asked anxiously.

"Just dis afternoon. Right in the middle of da noon rush. Seemed pretty fidgety to me. What'd he do?" the man asked.

"I can't answer that, sir. Thanks for your help, though," I said to him as I gave him the universal nod.

"Yeah, no problem. Anytime!" the man replied as he nodded back and returned to slicing meat.

While CSU was processing the warehouse, I thought I might as well head back to the station.

I walked into the station and to my surprise, half the detectives were gathered around Billings desk in the back.

I approached the group, pushing those in the outer circle to the side to reach the center attraction. It was a birthday cake. As if on cue, they all broke out in song as I approached the center.

"What the hell is going on?" I yelled.

One of the detectives responded, "We're celebrating. It's Billings' birthday! You want some cake?"

"No, I don't want any cake! No disrespect to you Billings, but there is a woman missing! Possibly murdered by some psycho! We need to be working this case day and night until we find her!" I shouted, heading to my desk.

As the crowd dissipated, Billings blew out the candles and went back to clacking his keyboard to look busy. The lieutenant was out this week and it was clear that when the cat's away, the mice will play.

I turned back around to face Billings and said, "I don't care what you have to do, I want a printout of every property for the entire Talon family NOW!" I was becoming more and more frustrated at the lack of progress in this case.

As I headed back to my desk, my phone started ringing. Leaping to catch it before it went to voicemail, I answered, "Solace here!"

It was a cop from the eighth precinct. Our BOLO was seen by an officer on the night shift. He had stopped someone who matched the description of the perp by the exit ramp for Tranquility Woods. He noticed the insurance and registration was not in his name, but the name on the license matched the guy we were looking for. He was about to check the trunk when he had to run to an *officer down* situation. But not before reporting what he thought he saw through the busted taillight. Something resembling a foot!

I hung up the phone feeling defeated. Had that been a dead body in that trunk? Was I too late?

Deep in thought, I was interrupted by Billings and another printout.

"What's up? You find anything?" I looked up and asked.

"Yes sir, I have the complete list of properties you asked for. And, I…well, sir…I just wanted to apologize about the party and all. We know our top priority is to find Ms. Romano," he stammered.

"It's okay, Billings. I may have overreacted a bit. This case is really getting to me," I said begrudgingly. "By the way, happy birthday."

I was reviewing the report and relaying to Billings the intel from the call I had just received from the eighth precinct.

There was one property that matched the location of Tranquility Woods. A well-to-do boating community where his father-in-law had a home. It was a five-hour drive, but it was our only shot at finding Ms. Romano. We might be able to get local New York police to assist by sitting on the house until we get there.

"Come on, Billings. It's going to be a long night," I gestured. "You might want to bring a few slices of that cake for the trip. Oh, and I have a quick stop before we hit the highway."

After I finished feeding Ms. Romano's cats and tending to the litter boxes, I was feeling more hopeful about finding her alive. I wasn't sure if it was for me or the cats, but either way, it would better for everyone if she was found alive.

"You usually take such a personal interest in missing person cases, sir?" Billings asked with a creased forehead.

"Not really. But I do have a soft spot for neglected animals. Or maybe it's just a case of the guilts. I feel like the killer has been one step ahead of us this whole time, just laughing at us. All while Ms. Romano could be in pain, suffering, or even…you know…" I mumbled, but couldn't finish.

"We'll find her, sir. Would you like me to drive?" asked Billings.

"Sounds good, sure. There's a book I've been meaning to catch up on," I replied, as I pulled out the latest novel in the Anna Romano series and smiled to myself.

CHAPTER 12

4 days ago...

Frederick Talon

My wife was beginning to get suspicious. Thank God this was the last day I had to hide Cat Lady in the garage. I managed to sneak a bagel and cup of OJ to her when the family left for a last-minute errand. Unfortunately, she was in a mood, and began screaming as soon as I removed the duct tape. Something about not hurting her, and promising not to tell anyone if I let her go home to her cats. I put a stop to it all mid-scream. Geez!

I told her to shut up, eat, and say her final prayers. She was so hungry, she did as she was told, shoving the bits of bread into her mouth hastily, like a squirrel hoarding nuts for the winter.

I couldn't care less about *who* or *what* she was leaving behind. She'd had a good life as a famous author. She was her own person and didn't have someone telling her what to think and do her whole life. I knew I had to make this right once and for all.

I reached into the trunk and grabbed the last of the supplies — the tarp.

I laid it out on the garage floor and attempted to get Cat Lady onto the tarp. She was going to make this difficult. I had to use more rope to bind her legs and keep her from kicking me. Well, she was determined to live – I'll give her that. However, the special gift I put into the juice should have her quieting down shortly.

Twenty minutes later, I got her wrapped up in the tarp and loaded her onto the golf cart to drive down to the dock and get her onto the boat. I covered the tarp with a blanket just to be safe. This was the final step.

I called my wife to find out where they were and how much time I had left. They were in the store trying to decide which brand of sun block to purchase and then had to pick up snacks. I had another half hour at most.

Now, if I could only get this stupid silencer attachment onto the gun and finish taping the explosives in bundles, so they would be ready for me to attach to the underside of the boat. No one would ever believe I was this brilliant. I'll shock them all. I'll be the talk of the town. No one will take advantage of me EVER AGAIN. People will remember MY name. Frederick Talon, the great Houdini, a REAL man who knew how to take care of his family.

Once again, I ran through the checklist in my mind:

Drug Cat Lady…check!

Move body to boat…check!

Prepare the explosives…check!

Disappear…check!

I was ready to head for the boat when I realized I forgot a step. Damn!

I hopped off the golf cart and opened the deep freezer in the garage. I lifted the two small body bags up and into the small compartment in the back of the golf cart. Thank goodness this was one of the larger models.

I hit the gas and headed to the dock, waving at neighbors casually as I sped by, as if I was *not* transporting bodies in the back of my cart – dead and alive.

Once the coast was clear, I used a dolly to get all the bodies down below and covered up, making sure I poked a hole in the tarp for the one that was still alive.

It was a massive boat owned by my father-in-law. They say size doesn't matter, but I swear he's compensating for something in every purchase he makes. Ridiculously large trucks, homes, buildings, you name it. It's sickening. His whole life he had everything he wanted — born with a silver spoon in his wide, obnoxious mouth. And he gave his daughter so much that ANY poor sap that came along would never be able to compete with what Daddy provides. As it happens, I wound up being that poor sap. For now. Until tomorrow. Then he would be the poor sap. And I would be the MAN ON TOP.

Now that the back room was locked up, there was only one thing left to do — get the whole family onto the boat and head for the food festival on the other side of the harbor.

I hopped back into the golf cart and headed up the hill to the house…just as the family was pulling up.

"Daddy, Daddy…look what we got!" his boys shrieked with joy.

CHAPTER 13

Still 4 days ago...

Anna

It is my second day in this crummy garage. My arms and legs are stiff and sore, and the gag has been replaced by duct tape, which is chafing my mouth and face. What in the hell is this guy planning to do with me? If he wanted me dead, he certainly could have killed me by now! I'm also so worried about my babies. They must be hungry and scared.

I can hear the voice of young children, but I can't imagine he would bring me into the same house as his family. What if his wife came in? Maybe she's not a factor anymore. Maybe he already got rid of her.

I hear footsteps. He's coming.

I prepare myself by holding my breath as he ripped the duct tape off. As soon as it was off, I screamed and started pleading my case again, but to no avail. He quickly punished me with a backhand to the side of my face.

He then screamed at me to shut up and threatened to take away my meal if I didn't settle down. So, I did. I was starving.

Time for my regular meal of bread and water. In this case, a bagel and orange juice. Not bad. At least he's feeding me at all. It tells me he has some kind of heart and he's not a total cold-blooded killer.

As I ate, I heard him mumbling something about rich people being born with a silver spoon in their mouth, and finally being 'the man'. He also said something derogatory about me and my cats. So rude! If I ever get out of these restraints mister, you just wait and see! I was stewing as I hungrily stuffed carbs into my mouth. There goes my girlish figure. Ha!

It's so funny, I had plenty of sleep last night, as uncomfortable as it was, but for some reason I'm beginning to feel very sleepy… "Oh crap. Not…again…noooo."

CHAPTER 14

3 days ago...

Anna

Uggghhhh. These drugs keep getting the better of me. I don't care how hungry I am, I'm NOT giving in again. I'm drenched in sweat, can hardly breathe, and my head is killing me. And why do I feel like I'm swaying? Oh no! Am I on a cruise ship? I've always wanted to go on a cruise…but not like this! Gosh, I would die for one of those shrimp fountains right now. With a gallon of cocktail sauce. Or maybe one of those chocolate fondue fountains. I can't think of food right now though, I've got to focus and get out of here. I hear voices from above, like children laughing. Maybe they can help me get free and call the detective. I really hope he hasn't forgotten about me. He probably has some hot cop lady girlfriend occupying his time. Not even working on my case at all! Oh well, who needs him. I can do this on my own, right? …WRONG! Who am I kidding? I need help in the worst way.

It seems like the sweat from being wrapped in this ungodly tarp loosened my hand restraints. Just a few more tugs and…ahh…freedom at last. Now for the dreaded duct tape rip. The good news: I probably won't have to wax my upper lip for a month after this! One…two…three…yowwwwwwww! That wasn't so bad…I guess.

I peeled the tarp from my upper body and was looking around for something to cut the knot in the rope around my feet. I spotted a tackle box across the room and decided to relive my childhood and inchworm across the room to it. What was that hanging out of the closet? Looks like more tarp, but the smell was rancid. I opened the door just a sliver and the giftwrapped cadavers of two children fell onto the floor! Part of their faces were revealed and I could see the 'deadness' in their eyes. Ewwwwwww! I covered my mouth with my own hands to keep myself from screaming aloud.

What in God's name was this sicko up to?! Was all of this, the dead bodies, and my soon-to-be dead body, all part of the plan he was talking about to be the 'man on top'? Now more than ever I am praying the detective has NOT stopped looking for me. I paused for a second and finally realized that my life could end today. I would have contemplated this fact longer but the smell was becoming overwhelming.

I kept crawling, opened the tackle box, and hit the jackpot! I found a utility knife and began cutting frantically. Luckily, it only took a few minutes, but as I was cutting myself free, I heard a man's voice getting closer and something like footsteps on stairs. Could it be Red Head coming to drug me again...or worse? I was so nervous I dropped the knife. How could I be so clumsy at a time like this?! Ugh! I wriggled out of the rest of the ropes and as I kicked the last of the tarp off I also kicked the knife — halfway across the room and into a floor grate. Dammit!

Now what? I begin looking around for a weapon, and caught a glimpse of red in my peripheral vision, and turned to see the fire extinguisher hanging by the door. It was my only shot.

I could hear the footsteps getting closer.

I shoved the bodies back in the closet and wrapped my tarp with a few pillows and other odds and ends to make it look like my body was still inside.

Then, I positioned myself behind the door...and waited.

Just yesterday...

Frederick Talon

The past two days had been wonderful. Fishing, swimming, barbequing, board games, and lots of laughter. I was really going to miss these moments while watching my sons grow up. And even though she could be a royal pain-in-the-ass, I would miss the 'princess' too. Her family's money had given us a good life up until now. But, unfortunately, it also gave me access to enough funds to hang myself in a chokehold of gambling debt higher than Mount Everest.

The family was packed up and ready to go. I hugged my kids and kissed my wife passionately for the last time. She gazed at me strangely, as it had been years since she'd felt any passion at all from me. She knew the time had come and a look of uncertainty washed over her porcelain skin for just a second before she straightened up and returned to her normal stoic look of strength.

No one turned to watch him descend to the lower deck of the boat. The detonator had remained in his pocket all morning. During breakfast, his trigger finger was itching to set it off and end it all right then and there, but he practiced restraint.

I am now in control. The man on top. Daddy-in-Law would never see his precious family again. Serves him right. I had devised the perfect plan. When the small explosion occurred, they would already be far away and safe. And, of course, left behind would be a hysterical grieving husband that just managed to escape within inches of his life; all the while grieving the loss of his entire family to a horrible tragedy. I would collect the insurance money at a reasonable time (not too soon as to arouse suspicion) and then meet up with my family in one year on a remote island off Cabo. My gambling had cost me everything and borrowing from the wrong people had proven near fatal. It was time to make it right. I could feel the detonator burning a hole in my pocket, just like those chips used to as I headed to the blackjack tables. Soon there would be a similar hole, burning into the bottom of Daddy-in-Law's precious boat.

As if walking towards my final sentence down the halls of death row, I descended the steps just as slowly. I turned the key in the lock and entered the small room used mostly for storage, and mentally prepared myself for the performance of a lifetime. I looked around and all the bodies were in place and ready to go, and a good thing too because the smell was getting pretty bad. Cat Lady hadn't moved a bit. The explosives were locked in a closet two doors down in another room. I decided to pause for a drink as a final toast to my master plan. I grabbed the whiskey from a nearby compartment and was about to take a swig when I felt a harsh crack against the back of my head. What the…?! My vision was fading in and out, while the blood ran down the back of my head and onto my neck.

Through the pain, I turned slightly to see my attacker was Cat Lady! She had gotten free somehow! I had to end this now. If we all had to die, so be it.

I reached into my pocket, flipped off the safety… and pressed the button.

CHAPTER 16

Present Day

Anna

He's here! Oh my gosh, he's here! This is my final shot. I have to physically attack this man who has kidnapped me and made my life hell for so many days. Breathe…inhale…hold it…now exhale…

He hasn't noticed I'm gone and seems to be smiling to himself. He's getting a drink, now's my chance! I swung as hard as I could and…THUMP! I conked him on the head good with the extinguisher. The pool of blood pouring from his skull let me know I hit him hard. He was swaying back and forth, and seemed to be fading, when he glanced back and saw my face. I heard him whisper, "No, not you. My plannnnnn." I just backed away, dropped the fire extinguisher in shock of all the blood. I had never caused another person physical harm in my entire life.

He was frantically trying to get his hand into his pocket for some reason.

I realized why when I heard a loud explosion from another part of the boat.

We both lost our balance and hit the floor hard. Red Head was knocked unconscious and my eyes were stinging from the smoke which was now pouring in from everywhere. I had to get off this boat…NOW!

I ran out the door, up the steps, and into the sunlight. Flames were shooting up from everywhere and I knew my only choice was to jump. I held my breath and leapt off the edge of the boat, thinking to myself how thankful I was to my mother for pushing me into joining the swim team in high school.

For some reason I yelled 'Cannonball!' as I dove to safety and splashed into the cold water. As the water washed around me, the sting of the rope burns began to set in and I winced a little from the pain. I had to ignore it for now, swim to safety, and find help.

In the back of my mind, I was feeling somewhat guilty about the death of my kidnapper. Red Head wasn't a nice guy, but I didn't wish death by explosion, or even blunt force trauma, on anyone. Detective Solace was not going to believe any of this.

I was coming up to the shoreline and I could see a large crowd of people talking, laughing, dancing and eating. As I crawled ashore, a big sign welcomed me to the Annual Harbor Food Festival. Maybe it wasn't too late for me to get some shrimp after all.

Everyone stopped to stare at the soaking wet woman who just came ashore in the middle of their food festival. I couldn't care less about the stares as I went into *survival panic mode*.

I lunged at the first person I made eye contact with and tried to convince them to call the police or let me borrow their phone.

I yelled randomly, to anyone who would listen, that I was kidnapped and held captive for the past few days by some lunatic who thinks one of my books was about his life! He was insane! Did no one see that boat just blow up? Hellooooo?

After not being heard or believed, I had to take matters into my own hands. I spotted a vendor away from his cart, engrossed in a conversation with a friend. So, I used the opportunity to jump on his bicycle ice cream cart and take off! Screams of "Get that lady!" and "Stop her!" attacked me from behind. I yelled back that I had to get to the police and would return it as soon as possible. I pedaled as fast as my legs could possibly go after all I had been through.

I was gaining momentum motivated by my desire to see my babies, and maybe a little from my desire to see the detective in swim trunks rubbing oil all over his broad chest…but that's beside the point. No time for daydreaming now!

I had my bearings now and knew where I was from the road signs. I was a long way from home for sure, and was in for quite the journey. If I had money I could head to a bus or train station. Maybe I'll try to get to the closest police station and get a ride from there.

Now entering the highway, there were cars honking, passengers and drivers pointing, and angry road rage candidates. All of these individuals were apparently trying to get on YouTube or the evening news by running after the soaking wet, little Italian woman, riding an ice cream bike cart off the road.

I began thinking about how cold I was, and about how I should have stolen a towel and jacket from the festival, when I was almost clipped by a motorcycle.

I flipped him the bird and just kept pedaling. Since there was no *ice cream bike cart* lane per se, I tried to stay in the right lane or as far right on the shoulder as possible.

Just then, I heard laughter and cackling. "How much for a cone, sexy?" "Where's the wet T-shirt contest?"

Wet T-shirt contest? Oh, I get it. I'm wet and freezing cold at the same time, hence the enticing top view. I'm all but flattered at this point.

The motorcycle gang off to the left continued to taunt me and were moving closer to my 'lane' and getting more aggressive. Seriously, right now? This is the last thing I needed.

I was definitely feeling a bit nervous about the noises and gestures getting closer and closer to my 'bike cart' personal space. Then, the sudden swerve of one of the motorcyclists into my lane with an outstretched hand startled me.

It startled me enough to make me lose my balance. And yes, I swerved off the road. And yes, I fell. Down a hill. A hill that ended in a drainage system.

The cart was ruined and I now smelled like sewage water. I could go for a cone right about now, but with the heat, the ice cream was probably soup, (not to mention possible covered in sewage), which was certainly no good to me at this point.

Time to head back to the highway. I started climbing the same hill I just fell down in search of a new good Samaritan. Damn bikers.

* * *

I never thought I would be type of woman to hitchhike, but at this point, what could happen to me that hasn't already? My T-shirt was no longer soaked, so I didn't have sex appeal working to my advantage anymore. The rest of me looked dirty, worn out, old, and beat up.

I was wondering what the detective would think seeing me in this condition, when a car pulled over and rolled down the window.

"Hey, you need some help?" the young girl asked in between smacking some type of fruity gum. I could smell it from the window.

"Yes, thank you so much! I'm trying to get to the local police station. Can you give me a ride?" I asked anxiously.

"Oh wow, yeah, so I'm like totally late for class. I take classes at the local college. But I can totally give you a ride to my exit up ahead and call you an Uber to take you the rest of the way. Is that cool?" she asked as she popped another bubble.

"That would be totally awesome…I mean cool…thank you!" I responded, trying to blend in. The furrow of her brows indicated I had it all wrong. She probably gave that look to her mom all the time. "If you give me your contact information, I will pay you back as soon as I get back home."

"Um yeah, sure, no problem," she responded as she turned the radio back up to level 'deaf-by-25' and haphazardly merged back into the highway traffic.

I was hoping I would make it to the exit alive.

She threw her phone at me and told me to open the Uber app and enter my destination. We would be at the college entrance bus stop in five.

I thanked her for being so kind and reminded her I would be paying her back in full ASAP. I stepped out of her car just as the Uber was pulling up.

"Later dude," I whispered under my breath and waved faintly, as the Uber pulled off towards the police station.

Again, no one is EVER going to believe this story.

CHAPTER 17

Diving for Survivors

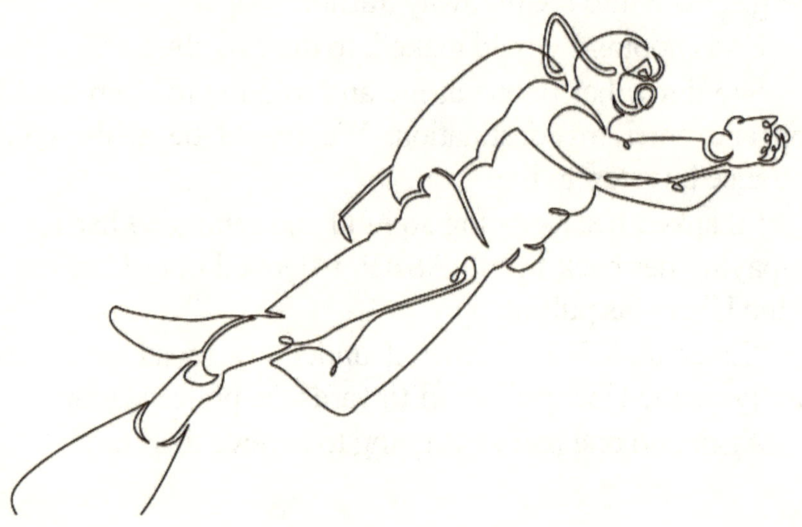

Detective Solace

We just pulled up to the entrance of Tranquility Woods as I was wiping the sleep out of my eyes from a quick nap. Time to snag us a kidnapper.

The rest of the units pulled in behind us and SWAT was already out front when we arrived.

The guy leading SWAT was an old friend from the academy, Jose Rodriguez. I greeted him with our usual "Que pasa?" and bro handshake from the good ole days and showed him our warrant.

Other niceties had to wait until after the raid…there was a hostage involved and she needed us.

We were in position and ready from the front, sides, and back of the home. Neighbors were starting to become curious and gather outside their homes, but patrol kept them at bay.

"Move in!" Jose barked. My team was right behind them.

Once again, there were "clears!" heard from inside the house after each room was checked. And once again, this guy was one step ahead of us.

Jose called me from the garage to look at something. He found the same materials they found at the warehouse in the garage: duct tape, rope, drugs, and this time, there was also tarp. Not a good sign.

Where in the world is this guy? And his family? Is our victim even alive?

"Let's start canvassing the neighborhood again. Maybe another neighborhood watch guy knows or saw something," I instructed, as I turned to Billings and shrugged.

"Actually, it looks like he found us. Look, boss." He pointed towards the crowd of neighbors out front with patrol holding them back. There was a man flagging us down vehemently.

"Come on, let's see what he wants," I said to Billings. "Hope you have your notepad and pen ready," I chuckled jokingly.

"It's about time. Geez! Excuse me, sir! Official police business here!" the heavyset man in a robe and slippers ordered the officer guarding the perimeter to let him through, but the officer wasn't budging.

"It's okay officer, he's with us," I said almost amused.

Neighborhood Watch guy obviously felt 'special' and gave the officer letting him through an 'I-told-you-so' look up and down before strolling past the blockade.

"So, what do you have for us, Mr…?" I asked slightly intrigued by his persistence. Billings was ready to takes notes, pen in hand pressed onto his notepad.

"Mr. Jack McNabb at your service!" he boasted proudly.

I told him we would appreciate any information he could provide about his neighbor's whereabouts and waited for him to start blabbing. Based on this man's high energy and the amount of coffee on his undershirt, I imagined Billings would need an additional notepad.

"I saw him just last night. Always in that garage tinkering with this and that all hours of the night. I thought it was VERY suspicious," he said. "And his wife just went out with the kids yesterday."

I asked him if anything was suspicious about today.

"Well, actually, I thought you were here about the boat explosion on the harbor. You didn't hear about it?" he asked.

"Boat explosion? Wait a minute! Billings, we didn't check the pier!" I gasped as I smacked my hand to my forehead.

"Jose! Jose! Can we get some men down to the pier? It's out back behind the house."

Jose yelled back across the front lawn, "Just got the call from Harbor Patrol. There was an explosion on the harbor. It may be Talon's. His boat is missing from the dock. A man and two children were found in the debris. Not sure if there are any survivors yet."

"Thanks Jose! I'll meet you down there in a sec!" I yelled back. A man and two children, but no woman. Where was Ms. Romano and Talon's wife?

This isn't good at all. Billings and I dismissed Mr. McNabb and guided him back behind the blockade.

Ms. Romano is nowhere to be found, but we know she was being held in the garage, even though CSI is still processing the scene.

I hope to God **someone** survived that explosion, I thought to myself, as I walked down the hill to the dock.

Everybody Fall to the Floor

Anna

I was covered in dirt and exhausted by the time I reached the precinct. I was now limping and I struggled to find the right words as I approached the front desk. "I need to speak…to find…Detective..." A loud thump. I was later told that I hit the floor…hard.

"Somebody call a bus! Quick!" an officer shouted.

I was in and out, but I do remember the sound of the sirens and the ride in the ambulance…vaguely.

The paramedics rushed me to the nearest hospital.

"Let's get her to x-ray, STAT! We are checking for broken bones and a concussion. Do the MRI first!" the ER doctor called out to the staff rushing me in from the ambulance.

Hours later, or maybe a day later, who knows, I was slowly opening my eyes to the gray/beige colors of a standard hospital room. A tray was pushed to the side of the bed and held crackers, a water pitcher, a plastic spoon, and a cup of green jello.

I was beeping from three different units and none of them made the monotone sound of a flatline. I'd made it, thank God! There was an IV in my arm connected to a drip bag on my right, so I guessed I wouldn't starve. I was thinking how difficult it would be to shove cannoli into that skinny tube when a friendly southern voice interrupted my thoughts of hunger.

"Well hello, sleepyhead. So glad to see you're awake. How ya feeling?" the nurse who miraculously appeared in the doorway asked. Or maybe she had been in the room all along, who knows?

"A bit groggy, thanks," I responded slowly with a raspy voice I didn't quite recognize.

"Well, that's expected. You have quite the concussion, a ton of scratches and bruises, and a sprained ankle! What in the world happened to you, darlin'?" she inquired with a wrinkled forehead of concern. "You were mumbling somethin' about a bike with ice cream on a boat with a lot of cats. No one could make out a thang you were sayin'," she chuckled lightheartedly.

"The last thing I remember was pulling up at the police station. I wanted to get in touch with Detective Solace," I mumbled.

"Well sure sweetie, there's a detective right outside your room. He's been waitin' for you to open those pretty little eyes of yours, so he could get your statement," she sang. "Let me fetch him for ya."

She disappeared as fast as she had appeared, and a moment later, an officer was standing in front of my bed.

"Afternoon ma'am, I'm Officer Maddox. I called for the ambulance to bring you here after you lost consciousness down at the station. I can take your statement now if you'd like," he said warmly.

"Thank you so much for your kindness, Officer Maddox," I said. "I'm actually an active kidnapping case, or at least I hope I am still active, with a Detective Solace in New Jersey. He's familiar with my case and I need to let him know that I'm okay. Also, I really need to get back to my cats," I rambled.

The confused officer nodded and left the room, confirming my request to locate Detective Solace, with a "yes ma'am" and "right away ma'am."

I pushed the nurse button and waited for assistance. The pack of crackers and water pitcher were teasingly out of my reach. It wasn't a traditional Italian meal, but it would have to do for now.

I felt so naked without my phone. I wanted to let Shirlene know what had happened to me. Maybe after my traumatic couple of weeks with Red Head, Shirlene would grant me a month or two of no-nagging coupons. Whether I am late to an event, forget to respond to emails, or whatever other *faux pas* I make in the marketing and social media world, my coupons could act as my 'get out of jail free' card for all of them. A girl can dream, right?

The cheery, southern, and stunningly attractive nurse, was back to help me. "You rannnggggg," she sang, *way too cheerily*.

It was going to be a long night.

We Got a Live One!

Detective Solace

I was just arriving at the dock noticing the empty slip where Talon's missing boat was usually held, when someone ran up behind me and caught me off guard. It was one of Jose's men.

"Detective Solace! They may have found a survivor! They're headed in your direction now and we have medics on the way," he relayed excitably.

Excellent! I wondered who it could be.

I didn't have to wonder long as a speedboat with flashing lights was rapidly approaching the pier. The side of the boat read *Harbor Security* and a man was lying on the back seat, covered in blankets. Security staff all wore white polos with the same *Harbor Security* black lettering. The driver was focused on carefully docking, while the other staff member was comforting our survivor in the back.

I approached the boat after it had anchored, introduced myself, let everyone know the ambulance was close by, and that I would take it from here, as this was an active investigation. I could see a middle-aged man with red hair, though half-singed, laying in the back of the boat covered in soot, second- or third-degree burns, perhaps, and soaked to the bone.

"Sir, please state your name for the record," I said firmly.

"Frederick Talon," he responded with a raspy voice in between fits of coughing.

It was the perp! The man who had caused so much chaos over the past few weeks.

"Well, well well...Mr. Talon. You have some serious explaining to do," I said coyly, in my best Desi Arnaz accent.

No one seemed to have gotten the joke, thereby showing my age, so I pressed on.

The ambulance was coming down the grassy hill and stopped just short of the dock. The EMTs and paramedics rushed out, stepping around me to get their transport onto the stretcher. They frantically addressed the burns with the antiseptic patches they had on hand, while also tending to the gashes in his head, probably from flying debris during the explosion. Although the blood on the back of his neck and shirt didn't match that scenario. Minutes later, they were lifting him onto the stretcher and loading him into the ambulance.

I yelled out to Billings and Jose, now standing on the back lawn talking, that I would be riding in the ambulance to the closest hospital, and then escorting the prisoner to our precinct in Jersey for booking. Billings confirmed he would head back and meet me there later.

The hospital staff and their transport looked up in awe at my use of the word 'prisoner'. I smiled and stepped into the back of the ambulance, sat down across from Talon, and pulled out my handcuffs.

"Congratulations, Mr. Talon, you win the criminal-of-the-year award…a pair of matching bracelets!" I said sarcastically as I connected his left hand to the stretcher. "Oh, and you also have the right to remain silent. Anything you say or do can be used against you…"

* * *

It had been a long day and the lull of the ambulance *could* have put me to sleep, if it was not for the incessant questions that were rustling around in my head. When Talon was coherent, I shot my questions his way in quick succession before he lost consciousness again.

Where is Anna Romano?

Where is your family?

Were those your children that were found in the boat debris?

Where is your wife?

By the time we arrived at the ER, I had learned absolutely **nothing** about Talon's reason for grabbing Anna, the ID of the other two bodies found, or the whereabouts of his wife. Oh, what a tangled web we weave. Hmmmm, it also just now dawned on me, I'd been calling the victim, Anna. When did I start identifying with her on a first-name basis?

I was stepping out of the ambulance and walking towards the ER when I ran into Officer Maddox, chugging down coffee like water and smoking a black and mild. We were good friends during our academy days. A soft-spoken, timid man, with a wife and kid here in New York. I never could understand why he chose the beat, but he was a good cop, fair and honest.

He looked up, as if he just recognized me from a lineup, and stomped out the cigarette quickly. "Hey, Detective Solace! I've been trying to contact you!"

"I can see that from the intensity of your puffing on that cancer stick. When are going to give those things up, Maddox?" I asked with my arms out and shoulders shrugged. "They kill, you know?"

"Yeah, I know, I know, but seriously, I was just taking a quick break. I've been on duty all day, sir," he said nervously. "As a matter of fact, I believe it's your case."

"My case? Which one?" I asked.

"Some lady named Anna Romano is upstairs, third floor, admitted a while ago, and said you know her case. Possible kidnapping?" he responded.

I jumped up, startled, and yelled, "She's alive? Oh my God, that's incredible! Listen, Maddox, I need you to stay with this suspect here. His name is Frederick Talon and I've got him cuffed to the stretcher. DON'T LET HIM OUT OF YOUR SIGHT!"

I ran, almost elated, for the elevators.

* * *

As soon as the elevator doors opened, I rushed straight to the nurse's station. "Excuse me, what room is Anna Romano in?" I asked the first nurse I saw.

"Room 312 right down the hall on the right," she answered.

For some reason, I had the urge to stop at a bathroom and check my appearance. I settled for just smoothing my shirt with my hands and tucking the loose parts into my pants in a rush.

"Detective Solace! In here!" a voice called to me.

I was so caught up in checking my appearance that I walked right past Anna's, *I mean Ms. Romano's*, room. It was her who was calling me.

"Oh, there you are, I was looking for you," I answered as I walked into the room with a smile.

She returned my smile as if happy to see me as well. I guess I would be happy to see me too, if I had just been through what she had.

"I'm so glad you're safe. We found Frederick Talon and he is under arrest," I said.

"He's alive? That's incredible," Anna said, somewhat perplexed.

"Well yeah, minor injuries, but I think he'll make it. Why do you sound surprised?" I asked.

"Well, I was on a boat when it exploded and he was um-er- incapacitated…by me…before the explosion…below deck," Anna mumbled.

"I'm sorry we took so long. We kept arriving too late at every location, and we, I mean I, took too long. I'm so sorry," I said with my head low.

"It's okay, Detective. I'm sure you tried your best," Anna reassured me.

"So, are you feeling okay?" I inquired.

"A concussion, some scratches and bruises, and a sprained ankle…but, I'm alive," she replied.

"And it's a good thing too! We're going to need your statement and testimony in court to put this guy away!" I said wholeheartedly. "Say, can you tell me who else was on that boat?"

"I was locked up below, but I do remember hearing children's voices above deck. Oh, I also found a body bag, wrapped in tarp, with two small corpses in it below deck when I was trying to escape! It was so gross, and the smell…Ugh!" she spewed the words so quickly she spat.

"But no woman's voice?" I asked with a furrowed brow.

"Nope. Why?" Anna asked.

"We don't have any leads on Talon's wife yet. And now that you've told me about the corpses, I'm not sure if his kids are alive or not. This case just keeps getting weirder by the minute," I said frustrated.

"Well, I am happy to help in any way I can. Maybe you can pull some strings and get me discharged early? Maybe assure them I will take it easy and get plenty of rest. The food is dreadful here, and I really miss my babies," Ms. Romano pleaded, batting her eyelashes and looking as helpless as one of her cats.

"Let me see what I can do," I responded, blushing.

* * *

"All set?" I asked, as I rolled the wheelchair into room 312.

"Yes sir! Ready to *roll*! No pun intended," she laughed aloud. It was a humble, comforting laugh that made me smile. She looked good in the police department sweatsuit I brought her to wear. Her other clothes were marked into evidence and sent over to the lab for analysis. I apologized for the sewage smell and told the detective I would explain later.

"The perp hasn't confessed as of yet, but I'd like to get your statement and the account of events down at the station right away. If that's okay?" I gently asked.

"Sure! Right after we make one quick stop," she winked.

Now That's Making a Statement!

Anna

I don't know which was more exciting, watching Detective Solace walk into my hospital room with that cute grin on his face, or pulling up to my house for the first time in days. His concern for me was obviously genuine. During the long drive back to Jersey, he told me all about breaking into my home while I was away to feed my babies. How romantic…I think.

Detective Solace opened my door, helped me out of the car, and handed me my crutches. I had no bags for him to carry, so he steadied me with a large, yet gentle, hand on my back.

He started to open the door when a voice from behind called out to me. "I see you're not missing anymore. Glad you're okay, Anna."

I knew, from the soft hum of the motor scooter, it was Mr. Craigly from across the street.

"Yes, thank you Mr. Craigly, I'm okay now," I responded as I half-smiled through my teeth. He was quite the *over observant* one, but I appreciated the concern, nonetheless.

"I thought this fella was a burglar or something, snooping around, but he said he was five-oh. I told him where to find the key. Was that okay?" he inquired, as if asking for reassurance and gratification at the same time.

"Yes, Mr. Craigly, he's one of the good guys. You did great," I replied. "I'll fill you in later, okay?"

He rolled off in a huff without so much as a goodbye. I guess he had more questions and was mad I was rushing him off. I'd smooth things over later with some cannoli.

Detective Solace continued opening the door, pushing it open with one arm while using one foot to block any getaway attempts by my babies. Tiny began jumping all over him right away and Bette was circling his leg. Awwww, they like him.

"I see they've taken a liking to you," I said slyly. "I can't thank you enough for checking in on them and caring for them while I was…um, er, away." For some reason, I couldn't find the word to describe my past status. I don't think I've truly come to grips with what happened to me. I've always used my sarcasm, humor, and writing to escape tough situations, but this was different. I actually could have been gone from this earth…*forever*.

"Ms. Romano…Ms. Romano…are you okay?" the detective was asking, snapping his fingers in front of my eyes to check my level of consciousness.

"Yes, yes, I'm so sorry. Zoned out for a moment," I said as I bent down to give all of my babies the attention they were so craving. I hugged and kissed every one of them while TatorTot licked my face repeatedly. Jasmine was attempting to jump from the top tier of one of the cat towers to the top of the entertainment center. Always putting on a show. Ha!

I headed for the kitchen to begin the chore of filling food and water bowls, and changing litter boxes. The detective was right by my side helping. The act of working together in silence was actually quite comforting.

When we finished, he asked if I wanted to freshen up before we headed out and I accepted the offer without hesitation. I bathed as best I could, considering the pain pills were beginning to wear off, changed my clothes, put on a new 'face' (as we ladies say), and grabbed my crutches to head out. The detective was sweeping up in the kitchen when I approached. Based on the white cream in the corner of his mouth, he had apparently found the leftover pan of cannoli in the fridge. I pointed to the 'evidence' on his face, handed him a napkin, smiled, and told him I was ready to go.

"Thanks. You're a great cook, and I was starving. Sorry," he chuckled. He wiped his mouth and locked up as I waved goodbye to my babies through the window.

I was ready to make the statement of my life, knowing it would take every ounce of my courage to get through it — every ounce of my courage to live through the minute-by-minute replay of the trauma all over again.

I had always been the type to diminish the work of shrinks, but I might be more open-minded once this whole nightmare is over.

We pulled up to the station and headed inside. Detective Solace was leading me towards an Evidence Lockup sign. "I think there's something you may like to have back."

As he strolled out of the gate, shutting it behind him, he handed me my cell phone. I never thought I would be so happy to see 32 missed calls in my life. My publicist Shirlene, my mom, and Bonnie had been worried sick about me. I'd touch base with everyone later. For now, the ringer would need to stay on silent.

That young officer who took my statement at my house after the break-in was walking up to Detective Solace.

"You're back, great! The suspect is here from the hospital and waiting for you in interrogation room 4!" Billings shouted excitedly. "And nice to see you in one piece, Ms. Romano! We could really use your help in nailing this creep!"

"That's what I'm here for," I murmured to his back, as he turned his attention away from me, strolling away as fast as he had approached.

I turned to Detective Solace and asked what hospital they had transported him from, and was shocked to find out it was the SAME hospital I was in. "Is that how you found me?" I asked him.

He laughed. "Something like that."

We were in a private interrogation room with cameras and recorders. Both were now flashing red to signal they were recording. The detective had his notepad open and pen in hand ready to write.

"Let's start from the beginning. When did you first meet Frederick Talon?" Detective Solace asked pointedly. This was the first time we had been alone and making direct eye contact. It was first time I noticed his eyes were green. I wiped away the slow-motion daydream that was coming into view and focused on my story. It was going to be a long night.

I began at the beginning: "Well, it all started at a New York book signing event. I had on a lovely floral-patterned dress and Shirlene was in rare form…"

CHAPTER 21

Speak Now or Forever Hold Your Peace!

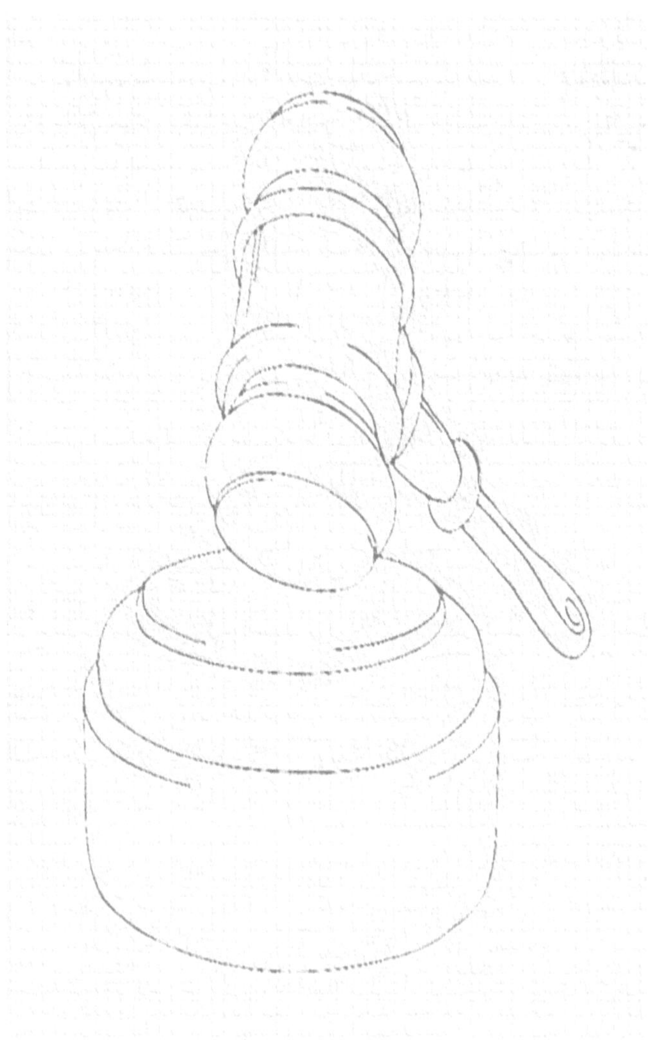

Detective Solace

Anna's stories were quite animated, so it took longer than expected to gather her statement. It was after midnight when I had a car drive her home, instructing them to make sure she was safe inside before leaving. She needed to rest. Although she tried to cover her emotions with humor, it was obvious going through the story again was painful for her. Now, it was time to turn my attention towards Talon.

I headed into the interrogation room ready to play the bad cop, but it seemed Billings had beat me to it.

"This is your last chance, Talon! Where is your wife?" he barked in Talon's face all while slamming his fist on the table with such force his coffee tumbled onto the floor.

This was getting ugly. I had to step in before he asked for a lawyer. I may be able to get something out of him before the lab results and his financials came in.

"Billings! That's enough! We don't browbeat prisoners around here! Take a walk and cool off!" I shouted. "Mr. Talon, I'm so sorry, please excuse my partner. How are you feeling?"

I started mopping up the coffee with a roll of paper towels I found in the corner of the room.

"Okay, I guess," Talon muttered almost trembling. "Is he always like that?"

"I guess you could say this case has all of us a bit wound up," I replied. "I'm sure you can understand why."

Talon put his head down and nodded in shame as I stood up and made my way to the trash can to dispose of the coffee-soaked towels. I was trying to judge his demeanor by his body language.

I sat down close to the suspect and whispered softly, "Listen Talon, you seem like a nice guy with a nice family. I don't know what happened to send you off the deep end, but you are facing some *really serious* charges here. I want to help you, maybe even put in a good word with the DA, but you gotta give me something."

Talon was beginning to break...sweating and wringing his hands. "I can't tell you. They will murder everyone I care about."

I moved in closer, close enough to count the beads of sweat on his forehead "They who? And what did the author, Anna Romano, have to do with *anything*?" I grunted angrily, trying to stay calm.

The suspect responded. "She knew too much. It was like killin' two birds with one stone. It became the perfect plan." His eyes lowered to his lap, almost in shame. It was unlikely Talon even had a conscience, but he sure knew how to play the role. He was shaking his head still looking down at his lap when my cell vibrated. A message from the lab. DNA was not a match to Talon. Those bodies were not his kids, which confirms Anna's story. I looked up from my cell and spoke again.

"We know the bodies on the boat were not your kids, Talon. If you don't tell us where the two cadavers came from and what you did to your family, you are facing life in prison. You are being charged with improper disposal of a corpse, *two counts*, and the kidnapping and assault of Anna Romano."

Talon lifted his head slowly. "I think I would like a lawyer now," he responded.

I stood up to leave the room. Turning to him one last time I answered, "That's your right Talon, but after this point there is absolutely nothing I can do for you. No deals, no leniency."

The suspect remained stone-faced and didn't utter another word.

I left the room and was headed for my desk when Billings approached.

He dove right in with the latest on Talon's financials, while waving the spreadsheet printouts in the air. "Looks like our boy has quite the gambling debt! And his bookie is affiliated with none other than the Bigly brothers. After he drained his wife's accounts, he turned to them to fund his habit. Talon racked up a $750,000 debt and you know they don't just let their 'clients' walk away scot-free. <u>They're going to hit every person you love until they get their money</u>. Talon may have just hidden his family somewhere because they were threatened," Billings reported. He seemed to have a renewed enthusiasm for the case.

He then went on to explain that the author was likely in the wrong place at the wrong time and simply wrote a book with the wrong storyline — just like I had suspected. As far as the explosion on the boat, her body would represent the wife's body and the two small cadavers would represent the kids. It was the perfect 'fake your death' scheme, except it was more like a 'fake your whole family's death' scheme!

Billings continued, "It could have been a fluke he survived, or maybe he planned to collect the insurance money and pay the Bigly brothers back the money he owed. Who knows?"

I interjected sternly, "Even if all of that is true, we STILL don't know if Talon disposed of his family or not. Keep searching! And while you're at it, let's verify alibis for the Bigly brothers."

"On it! Did Talon tell you anything, sir?" Billings asked.

"Nothing new, no. Everything he said was in line with what you just told me. Let's get an officer to stand guard outside the room. Also, bring a phone to our delightful prisoner so he can call his lawyer. It looks like the questioning is over for the night," I said, disappointed.

I was just about to sit down at my desk when my phone rang. It was Anna asking about the interrogation. I filled her in as much as I could without breaking protocol and told her I would touch base in the morning.

I doubted Talon would be talking even after his lawyer got here. He would probably be advised to cut a deal with the DA's office. We might as well get him to booking with the charges we knew would stick. I hoped Anna would be okay to testify in court. The kidnapping and assault would yield the longest amount of jail time, so we really needed her testimony.

I grabbed the paperwork from the printer and headed back to the interrogation room. As his lawyer hadn't yet arrived, dragging Talon downstairs to booking was supposed to be an uneventful task. It wasn't.

A gush of wind from behind let me know someone was fast approaching. I had only turned halfway around before I heard a bellowing voice.

"I'll kill you, Frederick! You hear me? Where's my daughter, you scumbag piece of trash? Where are my daughter and grandkids?" His voice barreled down the hallway with a large frame to match. For being so large though, this man wasted no time on his feet.

"Well, well, well, Mr. Moneybags Father-in-Law. Big Man, Jonathan Sturgis." The large man was fuming and probably about to do something he would regret, so I blocked Talon with my body and yelled for assistance.

Talon was smirking from ear-to-ear while mouthing off to his father-in-law. "Who's the big man now, huh Daddy Dearest? I AM! I'M THE MAN ON TOP AND THERE'S NOTHING YOU OR YOUR MONEY CAN DO ABOUT IT!"

Another officer ran over to help. He ordered Talon to shut up and escorted him to booking. Meanwhile, I subdued Mr. Sturgis and firmly escorted him outside. I informed him this behavior was not tolerated and could get him arrested.

"Listen, Mr. Sturgis. I know how upset you must be, but this is NOT the way to handle the situation. We are doing everything in our power to find your daughter and grandchildren. There's a chance they're hidden away safely somewhere. I assure you, we've been giving this case our full attention, okay?" I said calmly, yet firmly. "I would really hate to have to arrest a victim's parent."

"Why do you think they are being stowed away somewhere? The news said there were two small bodies on the boat, assumed to be children," he asked.

It was apparent he was confused and upset and would not leave without some type of explanation, so I added, "It seems your son-in-law had a gambling problem that got out of hand and he may have been trying to 'fake' their deaths to escape it."

"That son of a bitch! I told my daughter from the start he was no good! That's why I had her give him that pre-nup! Thank God I did! I could kill that bastard!" he shouted. Everyone in the parking lot turned to inquire about the ruckus, making sure their fellow officer was okay and didn't need assistance.

I put my hand up to let everyone know I was fine. "Mr. Sturgis, I need you to calm down. You cannot continue to make verbal threats like that. You should go home and let us do our job. Here's my card. If your daughter contacts you, call me right away, okay?" I looked him right in the eyes, with my left hand on his shoulder. "Can you do that for me, Mr. Sturgis?"

Mr. Moneybags nodded, apologized for losing his temper, thanked the police for doing a good job, and moped to his car like a scolded child who was unsure how to get into his parent's good graces again.

I wiped my brow and headed to the coffee shop on the corner for a pick-me-up. The station's coffee was *thick black sludge* that gave me chronic heartburn. I pulled out my cell to call the DA and fill him in on my way.

CHAPTER 22

Deceased and On the Run

Detective Solace

I was getting stares from everyone in the precinct, as they salivated over my fancy latte and coffee roll. I tried to ignore them as I strutted back to my desk…again.

I had a new pep in my step with the infusion of a double shot of espresso in my bloodstream. Also, after speaking to the DA's office, it looks like they will be going for the maximum charges. Arraignment was set for tomorrow morning.

Billings was on his way back from verifying the alibis of the Bigly brothers. He had texted me they were out of town for the past week in Chicago, with plane tickets and hotel receipts to prove it. Damn! Another dead end.

I was on my laptop typing up my notes in the Anna Romano case and chewing on my coffee roll, when my phone rang.

"Solace. Can I help you?" I said with my mouth full.

For a moment, the line was silent.

"Hello, is anyone there?" I asked, figuring this was probably just a prank from some bored kid.

"I…I need to speak to the detective on the Frederick Talon case. My name is Dominique…Dominique Talon."

I sat in shock not believing what I had just heard.

Dominique Talon and I only exchanged a few sentences, but as I hung up the phone, *everything* began to make sense. She and the children were safe, and our next priority needed to be exhuming the body of Talon's first wife, looking for an undetectable poison in the bloodstream, and following the money trail.

Dominique left me with the final words: "Oh, and tell Anna I will miss her, and thank her for believing in me."

Now I understood everything. The source of Anna's book was no longer a mystery. I would definitely be paying Ms. Romano a visit later this morning.

The sun was just coming up and I had been up for 36 hours straight. I only knew of one other department that worked the same crazy hours. I picked up the phone to make a call to the coroner's office. We had to exhume the body of Talon's first wife and run the tox screen again.

"My, my…you're up early detective!" Dr. Bernstein exclaimed quite boisterously from the other end of the phone line. I pulled the phone away from my face in case the energy was contagious. Boy, did I hate morning people.

"Actually, I never went to sleep. And you're quite chipper at the crack of dawn! What gives?" I asked, slightly annoyed.

"Well, unlike you, I DID sleep last night. And, had a long, hot shower this morning before coming in. Which is more than I can say about you! I can smell you all the way over here!" he laughed again exuberantly — *like a mall Santa Claus in December.*

It was a joke he used quite often, so I laughed along, as if it was the first time I had heard it.

After all the niceties, I explained what I needed, and to my surprise, he said a request had come in from a long-lost sister a few weeks ago. The strangest thing was that the initial report never mentioned the deceased having any siblings.

Dr. Bernstein continued, "I just got the body in the other day and ran another tox screen, and found what you detectives like to call the 'smoking gun'. Quite brilliant actually, *from a criminal's point of view*! A drug called digitoxin, completely undetectable, that mimics the effect of cardiac arrest."

"Is this something that could be ingested accidentally?" I asked. Now on the edge of my seat with suspense, coffee roll tossed aside beginning to harden into a state of staleness.

"Absolutely not! Not at these levels anyway. You know, some forensic scientists refer to this plant toxin as the 'perfect' murder weapon? I went ahead and changed the cause of death from 'natural causes' to 'homicide by poison' in the autopsy report and on the death certificate," said Dr. Bernstein.

"That's excellent news, Dr. Bernstein! I could kiss you right now! Thanks so much!" I shouted into the phone.

"No need for that, Detective. At least not until you've returned home and showered," he chuckled heartily.

I thanked him again and called the DA with the great news. They were able to add the murder of Talon's first wife to the list of charges before arraignment in a few hours.

I grabbed my keys to the squad car and headed home to freshen up before heading to Anna's. I was excited to see her, but also a little hesitant after having learned the full story of how she knew Talon's wife.

On the way home, I notified Billings of the call from Talon's wife, and instructed him to call off the search. I also filled him in on the new murder charges Talon was facing in the death of his first wife. We would have enough to get the death penalty, or at least life without parole.

Looking in the rearview mirror, I noticed I needed a shave. It would be worth the extra half hour to look my best. As I drove, I was thinking about Anna's relationship status, whether she was single or dating. My mind only snapped away from this thought as I drove up to my building.

Home sweet home.

The Truth Shall Set You Free

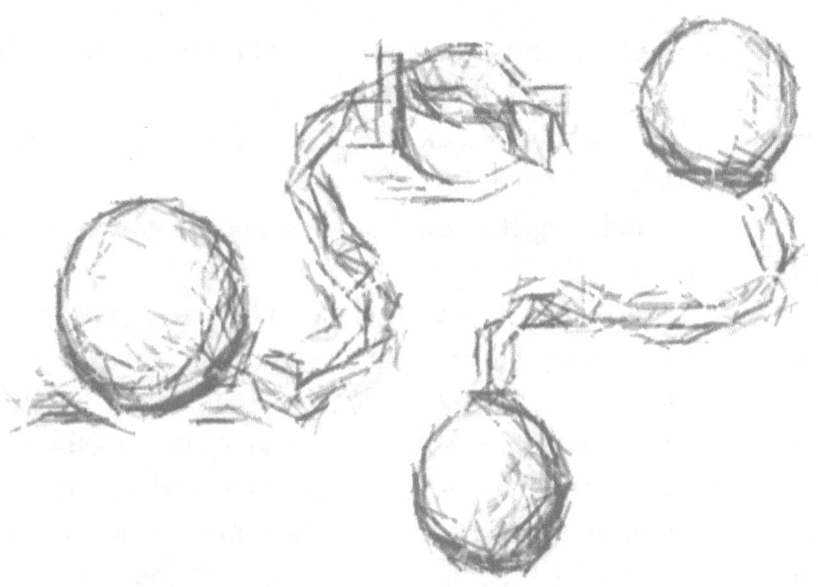

Anna

My cell phone was vibrating somewhere in between the couch cushions. When I finally dried my hands and ran from the kitchen to grab it, the noise had stopped and the icon for *missed call* shown on the Home screen. It was Detective Solace. I called him right back to see what he wanted.

"Hi, it's Anna. Anna Romano…sorry I missed your call!" I nervously rambled into the mouthpiece.

"Yes, I know," he chuckled. "I called you, remember?" Another chuckle.

"I was wondering if I could stop by and fill you in on the case?" he asked.

"Sure!" I responded. He said he would be here in 15 minutes. I hoped that was enough time to put on some makeup, fix my hair, and change my clothes! I must definitely like this man, I thought to myself. I don't do that for Shirlene or even my own mother!

I settled on my 'hippest' pair of jeans and my favorite flower print blouse just as the doorbell rang. Checking the mirror once more, I practiced a soft smile in the mirror and headed for the front door. I wanted to look happy to see him, not ecstatic (even though I kinda was).

"Detective Solace, so nice to see you again," I began, interrupted by his favorite feline friend rushing him at the door. "Oh! It looks like Tiny is happy to see you as well!" I exclaimed.

He bent down to scoop up his new best friend and give him a knuckle rub on the top of his head. "Hey buddy! How are ya?" he said happily.

He had such a warm spirit and loving smile.

I led him into the kitchen, offering coffee and a slice of coffee cake. He happily accepted.

"Have a seat, please," I said.

He proceeded to tell me, from start to finish, what had happened with the case, starting with the interrogation and the loud incident with the father-in-law during the booking.

I was managing a lot of oohs and ahs during the story all while dreaming about how I could get lost in those green eyes of his. I tuned back into his story, just as his eyes became even more animated with excitement.

"So then, after I thought *nothing else* could surprise me about this case, I head back to my desk and get a strange call. You'll never guess who it was!" he gestured, with his hands open.

I inquired with a spinning one-hand gesture insinuating "go on" and "tell me who" while nodding my head, and he continued.

"Dominique Talon," he said, while looking at my face trying to read my expression. It's what he was trained to do, and no doubt he was quite good at it, so I thought carefully about my next move. It was like Scrabble with only a few moves left. Do I play my high point letter now, or wait? Showing my hand could be dangerous. However, it was definitely time to show my hand to the detective. He deserved as much.

"That's wonderful! She's alive! So, what did she have to say?" I asked, while feigning shock.

"Yes, it is wonderful news," he continued. "I learned about Talon's first wife and how she really died. It seems she was poisoned with a drug that mimics a heart attack, and the coroner at that time completely missed it."

"We've since edited the cause of death to homicide and added that to the list of charges against him. If he cuts a deal with the DA, you won't even have to testify. We have all the forensics we need to put him away for life."

I just looked at him in amazement, hardly able to believe everything had worked out for the best.

"Oh, and one more thing," he added.

'What's that?" I asked.

"Dominique said to give you a message. That she will miss you, and to thank you for believing in her," he said with his eyebrows raised and head tilted.

The jig was up.

I just sat at the kitchen table with my mouth slightly open.

"I know everything, Anna. Why didn't you just tell me?" he prodded.

It was time to come clean. "I couldn't," I murmured. "I couldn't betray my source and put her life and the lives of her two children in jeopardy. I promised her that I would let the plan run its course, so that she and her kids could get away safely. However, I was never supposed to be a part of their story."

I explained to Detective Solace that Frederick Talon was more dangerous than anyone could imagine by starting from the beginning…

"Early on in their marriage, Dominique stumbled across a journal in the attic in some old boxes that belonged to her husband's first wife. He probably had no idea it existed. In it, she detailed the abuse by the hands of her husband and her declining health. She believed he had been poisoning her for months, but not sure why or how to prove it. Was it in the tea he brought her every morning? Or perhaps the wine he poured her in the evening? While researching credit card receipts, she found a receipt for Foxglove (also known as Digitalis purpurea) from an internet supplier in Canada, but it was too late. She died the next day. Dominique checked her last diary entry and the date of death on the funeral program and confirmed it.

She knew she had to find a way to expose the truth and get away safely with her children. Frederick would never let her go without a fight. He was an evil and sadistic man who had spent his life in a vengeful state of anger. You see, Dominique had learned that there were two sides to her husband: good and evil. On the outside, everyone saw him as a calm and gentle family man who doted on his family. But on the inside, he was an angry and spiteful man.

So, when he came to Dominique with this plan to escape his gambling debts, she went along with it. She had discovered the empty accounts the day before and was petrified of her husband trying to dip into the children's trust funds.

He was all tears and remorse as he told his story of a weak, pathetic man who found consolation in gambling, but was not very good at it. He said that the only way to escape the men he owed money to, was to fake the deaths of her and the children. He would take the insurance money after filing the death certificates, pay them off, and then disappear. It was the perfect plan...until one day...

One day, while setting the GPS for his favorite casino, her husband noticed an unfamiliar entry in the previous destinations list. Being the paranoid man that he was, he noted the address in his phone to check later.

The next day at his office, he ran a search on the address, thinking his wife may have been having an affair. It seems it was a woman who owned the property. Me.

He remembered seeing my name on a credit card receipt while paying the bills one month and put two and two together. The purchase was from a local bookstore; my book title, "The Silent Kill"; and I was the author she had met with. Only Talon's deduction was that I reached out to his wife because I had figured something out while writing my book. He had it all wrong.

So that's when her husband's obsession with me began; and also, when I became a part of Dominique's story. She never intended for me to get hurt, and I don't blame her for any of it. I'm just glad they are all safe.

She ended up getting a new set of fake ID's and passports. I'm sure she was far, far away from here before she called Doc with the tip on the death of his first wife."

I inhaled deeply and exhaled with a sigh of relief. It felt good getting the truth off my chest.

"I hope you can forgive me for not breaking her confidence?" I asked, almost begging. I was looking him right in his eyes, asking for forgiveness.

"I understand what you did and why you did it, but a lot of man hours were spent on this case looking for the family we thought he murdered. You understand that, right?" he responded firmly.

I nodded my head, hoping he would not be slapping the cuffs on me from across the table.

"It just would have been nice to have this information up front," he said, shaking his head, apparently frustrated with me. "And when did you realize your stalker was Dominique's husband?"

"It was at the warehouse, before he moved me to the lake house. He was on his phone and I heard him say her name," I answered. "That's when I put it all together."

"Wow. Well, um…I'm going to need to take some time and mull this over, if you don't mind? I'm not saying you broke any laws, but it's just…just a lot to process," he said as he stood up to leave. Tiny had fallen asleep in his lap, so he laid him gently on the linoleum floor.

"Of course, I understand," I mumbled. I had finally met a nice man, and then ruined it by breaking his trust.

I walked him to the door and we said our goodbyes.

The Purrrfect Ending

Detective Solace

I can't believe I am doing this. I finally meet a nice lady and this is how we start our relationship?

Relationship. Why is that word so scary to me? Maybe because Martha was my everything. The light of my life. My reason for living. I never wanted to go on living after her death. If it wasn't for the job…

I was raised to believe in God and sent to Sunday school as a child, but for the life of me, I don't understand why God has to take all the kind, beautiful souls so early. I can still remember the day Martha and I got the first diagnosis; sitting in the doctor's office holding hands. Martha stayed positive all through chemo, right up until we got the second diagnosis. The chemo wasn't working and the cancer was spreading. She was gone three months later. I've been alone and grieving ever since. Even after a year, I was unsure of whether Martha would consider it adultery if I tried to date again. My life had gotten so lonely, with only the job to keep me occupied.

For some reason, I imagined her looking down on me with her head tilted to the side and finger scolding me. I was smiling to myself when suddenly I was startled.

"Night, Solace!" Billings yelled over his shoulder as he headed for the front door of the station, anxious to start his Saturday night no doubt.

"Night Billings! Don't break too many hearts out there tonight!" I yelled back.

The station was half full and I wanted to change and freshen up a bit in the locker room before heading out. This was going to be a tough night. Anna Romano seemed like such a nice lady.

I was driving extra slowly, and reached her house forty-five minutes after departing the station. I sat out front of her quaint house, in her quaint neighborhood. Trees, flowers, white picket fences, and happy people out walking their dogs, waving hello as they passed each other. I could definitely get used to this type of life. I could see why Anna missed it so much when she was 'away'.

I dragged my feet up the steps and eventually rang the bell.

Anna opened the door, all smiles, with an apron on and a dish towel in her hands. The smell of marinara sauce enticed me through the screen door. I closed my eyes for a brief second to get up the nerve to do what I came to do. It had to be done. I considered it a direct order from the man above.

She opened the door, welcoming me in and Tiny was there to greet me once again; up on his hind legs, paws reaching all the way up to my knees. I hoped she will forgive my intrusion into her life.

"I'm so sorry to drop in on you like this, Ms. Romano," I stumbled over my words. It had been three days since I walked out of her kitchen, unsure how to handle the new information I had discovered on the Talon case.

"No worries, Detective. Come in please, and call me Anna," she said as she smiled.

"Okay…Anna," I blushed. I had to stay firm and remember why I was there.

"I was just cooking up some manicotti. Care to join me?" she asked as she turned back towards the kitchen.

"Before you go, there is something I need to do," I told her. "Something that will be very hard for me, and took me a long time to make a decision about."

"I understand and expected as much. You're just doing your job," she responded, as she removed her apron, set it on the back of the chair, and folded her hands together neatly in front of her.

I stepped forward, looked her directly in the eyes, reached out to touch her arm with one hand, leaned into her face, and kissed her.

Anna. I said her name in my head as I kissed her long and hard. And she kissed me back, as she wrapped her arms around my neck.

Afterwards, she stepped back, eyes wide, and said, "Well, that's NOT what I was expecting! Whew! You are quite the kisser, Detective."

"Call me John," I said shyly. My face was flush. The hard part was over. Now I can begin to get to know Anna as a real person, and not a victim.

"Hope you're hungry…John. The manicotti is just about ready," she responded with a wink and a smile.

As we ate manicotti, Caesar salad, and garlic bread at the kitchen table, we laughed and talked about our lives and many interests. Anna was a fascinating and resilient woman.

She was just about to beat me in our second game of Scrabble when my radio squawked — *something about a disturbance at a bar downtown.*

Back to reality. Oh well. Maybe Tiny would miss me and I'd have to come back...real soon. Anna's was a home that made me feel welcome and wanted, and I hadn't felt that way in a long time. Not since Martha died a few years back.

I believe it is time.

I believe I am ready…to try again.

About the Author

Cheryl **Powell**, (writing under pen name Cheryl Denise Bannerman), is a multi-genre author of three successful works of fiction, a motivational speaker, and CEO. She resides in Orlando, Florida, where she runs a virtual Training and Development company, GC Learning Services LLC dba Learn2Engage, which she founded in 1996.

> *"My mother introduced me to books at an early age and encouraged me to not only read, but also write. I remember having my first poem published in a collective book of poetry at the age of only 13. And when my mother wasn't working, I would read her my short stories, soaking in her edits and feedback like a sponge. Even at an early age, I was searching for perfection in my writings."*

Through the trials and tribulations of her life, she has learned to heal through her writing. One of the few female authors to introduce topics of social concern within 'fictional' stories, her books draw from the most intimate life experiences and include characters who have been victims of child molestation and domestic violence, and who suffer from depression and various other addictions. For example, her second book, Words Never Spoken, which just won the 2018 Book Excellence Award, is a self-help, poetry, chapter-book about a woman who escaped an abusive relationship, and even includes self-reflection journal pages for readers to document their feelings and begin healing.

Her goal in life is to keep writing and continue helping victims of Domestic Abuse/Violence, Grief and ANON family groups, and Corporate Health and Wellness groups, to heal through words — encouraging them to 'write the pain' via journaling, and expressing themselves through short stories, songs, and poetry.

Book 2 of The Anna Romano Series

THE PROLOGUE

I had just pulled the lasagna out of the oven when my phone rang. It was Shirlene. She was checking on me again for the tenth time this week. I guess she was as surprised as me that I was tangled up in yet another criminal investigation. She knew how stubborn I could be, and wanted me to lay low and follow John's instructions to stay out of the investigation. I couldn't believe how stingy he had been with information on the case the past few days. It just didn't seem fair. I mean, I did find the first body. Geez.

"Don't mess this up! John is one of the good ones," Shirlene said as if scolding a small child.

"I won't, don't worry," I responded as I hung up the call.

Famous last words of a nosy Italian woman. Ha!

I wrapped the lasagna in my insulated food carry bag to keep it warm and headed for the car humming to myself.

I plugged the address I retrieved from my internet search to Sherman Atkinson's home and started on my way.

I was rehearsing what I was going to say to him when the GPS told me I had arrived at my destination. I pulled into the long driveway and stared up at the large two-story home in awe. I was gathering my bags in the front seat when Mark stepped out of the front door and headed towards my car.

I stepped out to greet him and he offered to help me with the bags.

"Oh no, I'm fine. Thank you. Just brought a little something to say how sorry I am about your mom. How are you holding up?"

"Okay, I guess. Just heading to a friend's house. My dad's inside. Thank you for the food, it smells great," he replied as he walked to his car and got inside. Such a polite young man, I thought to myself.

I waved as he pulled off and was startled to find Sherman Atkinson at the door watching.

"Mr. Atkinson. How are you? I was just dropping off a pan of lasagna for you and your son for after the funeral tomorrow. I know cooking is the last thing on your mind when these things happen. I'm so sorry about your wife," I said, a bit awkwardly.

"That's very nice of you, Ms. Romano, right? You were the one that discovered her body in the bathroom at the charity ball," he seemed to confirm and question at the same time.

I nodded with empathy. "Yes, it was such a terrible thing that happened to her."

"Aren't you also that detective's girlfriend?" he asked, as we walked to the door and he graciously took the pan out of my hands.

"Well, yes, but…yes, I am."

As we entered the foyer and walked towards the kitchen, I looked around at the beautiful designs. Marble floors, exquisite art, abstract sculptures… "Was your wife the decorator of the house?" I asked in awe. "It's so beautiful!"

"Yes, it was one of her many hobbies. She enjoyed collecting antiques and visited auctions quite a bit," he smiled to himself.

As he was taking the pan out of the carry bag, and placing it in the fridge, his cell phone chirped. Suddenly, his facial features changed, and he turned to me with a furrowed brow. "Why don't you tell me the real reason you are here, Ms. Romano."

Just then, my phone chirped.

John texted: *Hey. Where are you?*

I responded: *Don't be mad at me...dropping off pan of lasagna at Mr. Atkinson's house*

John replied: *He's a suspect in the murders. GET OUT NOW!*

John's text is the last thing I remember before feeling a cold knife pressed to my neck.

What Did You Think of Cats, Cannoli and a Curious Kidnapping?

First of all, thank you for purchasing this book, Cats, Cannoli and a Curious Kidnapping. I know you could have picked any number of books to read, but you picked this book, and for that, I am <u>extremely grateful</u>.

I hope that it added value and quality to your everyday life. If so, it would be awesome if you could share this book with your friends and family by posting to social media.

If you enjoyed this book and found some benefit in reading this, I would like to hear from you and hope that you could take some time to post a review. Your feedback and support will help me to greatly improve my writing craft for future projects and make this book even better.

Visit the web site at www.bannermanbooks.com for contact information.

I want you, the reader, to know that your opinion is very important to me and hope that you will check out my other works of fiction:

Title	Category/Genre
A Bloody Stiletto, Cold Lasagna, and a Bestseller	Book 2 of the Anna Romano Mystery Series
Words Never Spoken	Women's Inspirational/Poetry
A Killer's Reflection	Erotic Psychological Thriller/Serial Killer
Black Child to Black Woman	Women's Fiction/Urban Fiction/Family Saga

Where is Anna Romano? 

See if you can find Anna 7 times in the hidden object image below.